Justice (*jus' tis*) n. the rendering of what is due or merited

BACK SEAT TO JUSTICE

TIM BAKER

BLINDOGG BOOKS 2011

Other work by Tim Baker:

Living the Dream

Water Hazard

No Good Deed

Pump It Up

AUTHOR'S NOTE:

THERE ARE MILLIONS OF BOOKS OUT THERE AND I WOULD LIKE TO THANK YOU FOR CHOOSING THIS ONE.

FIFTY PERCENT OF THE PROFITS FROM YOUR PURCHASE WILL BE DONATED TO A NON-PROFIT ORGANIZATION CALLED "GOLDEN HUGGS RESCUE INC."

HTTP://WWW.GOLDENHUGGS.ORG/

GOLDEN HUGGS IS DEDICATED TO FINDING LOVING HOMES FOR DISPLACED, ABANDONED, OR STRAY DOGS.

I HOPE YOU ENJOY THE STORY AND I THANK YOU WHOLE-HEARTEDLY FOR SUPPORTING SUCH A WORTH-WHILE CAUSE.

"IF YOU PICK UP A STARVING DOG AND MAKE HIM PROSPEROUS, HE WILL NOT BITE YOU. THIS IS THE PRINCIPAL DIFFERENCE BETWEEN A DOG AND A MAN."

MARK TWAIN

Acknowledgements

I would like to extend my sincere thanks to the following people for their invaluable help in the creation of this book:

Cover design **Keri Knutson** (http://alchemybookcover.blogspot.com)

For allowing me to include their restaurant in my books - **Tony and Carolyn of The Golden Lion Café** in Flagler Beach, FL - (www.goldenlioncafe.com)

For reading and critiquing an early draft – Linda Honchell, my brothers Joe and Ted (the real Brewski), my sisters Jayne and Joann, Janet Amedeo-Aurelio and Darlene Pardiny.

For technical advice on handguns – **Tony Walker**; (www.tonywalkerbooks.com)

For providing invaluable help in the publishing process – Armand Rosamilia

(http://armandrosamilia.com/)

DEDICATION

THIS BOOK IS DEDICATED TO

DEBRA JOHNSON

AND

BRIGITTE RITCHIE

FOR THEIR SELFLESS DEVOTION

TO

MAN'S BEST FRIEND

~ONE~

The simple truth is sometimes life just isn't fair.

A lawyer friend once told him *'Steve, life is not fair, it's just legal.'*

Legal or not, it wasn't fair that he was sitting there with an empty glass while the barmaid was at the other end of the bar letting some young stud chat her up. If he wasn't trying to maintain a low profile he would have found a way to get her attention.

Unfortunately, that wasn't an option.

Rule number one when you're tailing somebody…don't draw attention to yourself, especially when there's only six people in the bar, counting yourself and the bartender.

The mark was an overweight, balding guy named Fred Cranston. His wife, Rhonda, was looking for enough evidence to prevent him from squirming out of alimony in the divorce.

Cranston sat on the opposite side of the oval shaped bar. The large-breasted woman on the stool next to him appeared to hang on his every word, as if he were dictating a cure for cancer, world hunger and hangovers. From what Steve could see, she was probably half of Cranston's age. Another great unfairness…how these middle-aged, fat, bald loudmouths managed to convince gorgeous, young women to even look at them, let alone sleep with them.

Cranston, like most marks, had no idea he was being tailed and even less of an idea that his wife was preparing to take him to the cleaners.

That was where Steve Salem, former Boston cop, now a private investigator in Flagler Beach, Florida, came in. He made a comfortable living thanks to people who refused to play by the rules—which didn't seem fair either, but it was legal.

Not that he had any room to talk; his career with the Boston PD had been terminated prematurely for nearly beating a suspect to death—a flagrant rules infraction, but Steve didn't see it that way at the time.

When you crash through a door and find a twenty six-year-old asshole torturing and sodomizing a wheelchair bound girl not even eleven years old yet, the rules take a back seat to justice.

What he did wasn't legal, but in his mind it was fair.

The Mayor of Boston disagreed and because it was an election year, Steve became an example.

So now he was a P.I. tailing unfaithful spouses, insurance scammers and people collecting Worker's Compensation benefits while they worked another job under the table. It was good, low-risk money, but the constant exposure to life's down-side was exhausting and sometimes demoralizing.

Finally the barmaid worked her way to him and smiled widely.

"Another, Steve?" she asked.

"Yeah," he said, sliding the empty glass into the trough on her side of the bar, "thanks Dawn."

As he watched her pour Scotch into his glass he couldn't help but notice the way her shirt hugged the curves around her generous breasts. Her fiery red hair fell just short of her tanned shoulders and perfect white-as-snow teeth gave her smile the brightness of a lighthouse.

When she finished pouring his drink she set the glass on the bar, withdrew a tenspot from the stack of bills in front of him and walked to the register. Steve studied her form until she began walking back, at which time he forced himself to look her in the eyes.

The job wasn't completely without its perks.

Dawn returned to the young gun at the other end of the bar and Steve picked up his glass. The scotch, his second, went down smooth and warm. If the mark hung out here much longer he might have to switch to something non-alcoholic. A D.U.I. would mean he'd lose his driver's license, albeit temporarily, his P.I. license and his permit to carry.

Aside from Cranston, his girlfriend and the guy talking to Dawn, there was one other patron in the bar—a woman in her mid-twenties with the looks of a swim-suit model. Steve casually wondered what such a good-looking woman was doing in a hole like this, alone on a Friday night.

The door opened and three kids walked in laughing as they shook off the rain. They looked like they made the legal drinking age by minutes. The dim lighting in the bar made it tough to get a good look at them, but Steve thought he recognized one of them. They walked around the bar and sat next to the swim-suit model.

Testosterone strikes again, Steve thought.

Steve alternated his looks between his mark and the three kids. The familiar one was seated next to the woman and she screened Steve's view of his face.

The bartender put a draft beer in front of each kid and they all exchanged discrete conspiratorial looks, confirming Steve's suspicion they were under-age. One of them strolled to the electronic juke box and fed a bill into it. The relative quiet of the bar was assaulted by an obnoxious rap song, replete with references to whores, dead cops and drugs.

Cranston and his companion were getting cozy, nuzzling each other affectionately, oblivious to the pounding bass of the song. One of the woman's hands disappeared beneath the bar. The tell-tale motion of her arm, and the growing look of ecstasy on Fred's face, left little to the imagination.

Back at the other end of the bar, the three kids were getting a little rowdy. Two of them were standing and having an animated discussion about something. The discussion escalated into shoving and one of them bumped into the swim suit model.

As they apologized profusely, the one Steve thought he knew stood and walked quickly to the men's room.

Steve took a glance at Cranston—who was still enjoying the hand-job from his partner—then walked to the men's room.

Compared to the bar, the lighting in the restroom was bright enough to perform surgery. There was nobody at either urinal and one of the two stall doors was open. Steve saw the feet of the kid under the other door, standing.

Steve used the urinal then moved to the sink and washed his hands. When the kid emerged from the stall, Steve was drying his hands and checking himself in the mirror.

The kid walked toward the door but Steve backed away from the sink into his path.

"Aren't you gonna wash your hands?" he asked the kid.

"Huh?"

Steve's looked at their reflections in the mirror, his hunch was confirmed, he knew the kid.

"I said, 'aren't you going to wash your hands,' Brad?"

The kid's puzzlement increased.

"What? You know me?"

C'mere," Steve said, guiding the kid back to the stall and opening the door.

On the floor behind the toilet was a woman's purse.

"Pick it up," Steve ordered.

Brad paused before he complied, handing it to Steve.

"Now let me have whatever you took from it."

Brad sighed and dug into his pocket, handing Steve a few credit cards and a wad of cash. Steve read the name on one of the credit cards then looked at Brad.

"Her name is Valerie Casey, if you're interested."

Brad swallowed and blinked.

Steve stuffed the contents into the purse and slapped it against Brad's chest.

"Bring it back," he said.

"But..."

"Just drop it on the floor behind her stool. She'll think it fell when your buddy bumped into her. Then you and your two friends finish your beers and get the hell out of here and I won't have to tell your Uncle Ralph I saw you."

"You know my uncle?"

"Yeah, now, do we have an agreement?"

"Yeah."

"Atta boy."

Steve waited a few beats after Brad left before leaving. He took his seat and watched as Brad downed his beer then spoke to his friends. After glancing at Steve the other two finished their beers and they walked out into the rainy Daytona Beach night. A minute later, Valerie Casey left; Steve watched with an admiring eye as she walked to the door. When the door closed behind her he turned to check on Cranston.

"Damn it," he said.

Cranston and his mistress were gone.

Steve picked up his stack of cash from the bar, leaving half of his drink and a five dollar tip, and walked out.

The rain was coming down harder than it had been when he arrived and it was full-on dark now.

He sprinted to his Jeep, started the engine and did a slow drive around the parking lot looking for Cranston's blue Lincoln Continental. He was relieved, although not surprised to find it in a back corner of the lot, next to the dumpster—conveniently out of the sight.

Steve drove past and circled the building again. He found a place to park where he could inconspicuously observe the car and, if the rain let up, maybe even get some pictures for Mrs. Cranston.

He reached into the glove box and took out a digital camera, fitted with an f-2.8 zoom lens for low-light situations such as this. Unfortunately the lens did little to penetrate foggy windows.

There was very little activity in the parking lot, so the sight of approaching headlights from his right surprised him. The car looked like a Ford Taurus, probably a rental. It drove by Steve's Jeep slowly and proceeded around the building, its headlights hitting Fred Cranston's Lincoln on the way.

Salem watched with mild curiosity when the Taurus stopped just past the Lincoln.

Leaving the motor running, but turning the headlights off, a figure climbed out of the Taurus, cloaked in darkness and took a look around the parking lot. Steve began to get a bad feeling.

Dropping his camera on the passenger's seat of the Jeep, he reached inside his jacket for his .45.

The figure walked to the Lincoln and drew a gun.

Steve threw open the door of the Jeep and slipped on the wet asphalt. Stumbling toward the front of his car, trying to regain his balance, he heard three shots in quick succession. The gunman was in his car and gone before Steve could get close.

He walked through the rain and looked into the back seat of the Lincoln at the bodies of Fred Cranston and his mistress. Cranston sat with his back to the passenger's side rear door. His pants were bunched around his knees and his shirt was stained bright red from two bullet holes in his chest. His mistress was on her knees on the driver's side floor, her head, or what was left of it, still in Cranston's lap. The odors of sex and blood mingled and wafted out into the rainy night.

Steve re-holstered his .45 and took his cell phone out to call 9-1-1. While he waited for the call to go through he shook his head at Cranston and his mistress.

"Getting caught with your pants down is usually a metaphor, Fred," he said.

~*TWO*~

Saturday morning Steve caught up on paper work at his office, a converted beach shanty on A1A. After two hours of balancing the checkbook, paying bills and filing client reports he needed fresh air so he changed clothes and went for a jog on the beach.

When he returned to the office an hour later he checked his phone for messages then showered. As he stepped from the shower onto the vintage-fifties, white and black floor tile, he remembered his gym bag containing a towel and fresh clothes—still on the chair in the lobby.

"Oh, well," he said as he walked naked to retrieve it.

Timing is everything.

Just as Steve grabbed the handle of the bag, the door opened and Rhonda Cranston entered the foyer. Their eyes locked and the only sound in the room was the dripping of water on the laminate wood flooring.

Rhonda blushed and quickly turned to face the still open door. Steve recalled his words at the scene of Fred Cranston's murder about getting caught with your pants down.

"Talk about irony," he said.

"I'm sorry?" Rhonda said.

"Nothing," he said. "I'll be right back.

Steve returned shortly wearing jeans and a Beatles tee-shirt. Rhonda sat in one of the lobby chairs gazing absently out the window. The remnants of a long and emotional night were visible on her face. He invited her into his office where they sat on opposite sides of his desk.

"Okay," he said, "my apologies for that. How are you holding up this morning?"

She looked at him through puffy, red eyes.

"I don't know," she said. "I mean…a cheating husband is one thing, but this..."

Steve nodded, but didn't interrupt.

"I was ready for a messy divorce if it came to it. On the same token, part of me was clinging to hope that it wouldn't have to be that way, that you wouldn't find anything about his affair, but…" she shook her head and let out a small ironic laugh. "I guess I won't have to worry about that now."

"I'm sorry you have to go through it."

"I've been up all night, since they told me. I went to the morgue this morning to identify his body. Then to the police station for more of the same questions they asked me last night. It's like they think *I* did it."

Steve didn't mention the fact that, as the spouse, she was automatically high on the suspect list.

"Would you like some tea?" he offered.

"No thank you," she said, "I only stopped to talk to you about your investigation."

"I understand," he said, "I'll total up my time and expenses and refund the balance of the retainer."

She waved a hand and shook her head.

"No, that's not what I meant," she said. "I want you to keep going."

"Keep going?"

"Not with the infidelity, that's moot now. I want you to investigate his murder—I want you to find out who did it."

Steve was confused on a couple of levels.

"The police will investigate the murder," he said.

"I know they will, but they have other cases, it won't be their top priority, and besides, if they think I did it they'll be wasting time on that, time that could be used catching the real killer."

"And I certainly don't mean any disrespect, but last week you hired me to collect evidence of your husband's infidelity. Why would you want to hire me now, to find his killer?"

"I'm not sure to tell you the truth," she said. "Like I said, I was never *completely* ready for a divorce, there's always hope. So now maybe I just need closure. Will you do it?"

"If you're sure."

"I'm sure."

"I'm going to need more information about him, things I didn't necessarily need before," Steve said as he took a yellow legal pad from a drawer.

"I figured as much," she said. She produced a small manila envelope from her purse. "I brought a few things that may be helpful."

From the envelope Steve took out an address book/planner, a few photographs, a cell phone bill, some credit card bills, several months' worth of bank statements, a schedule of little-league baseball games, an invitation to a college reunion and a hand-written list of major league baseball teams—each followed by a number in parenthesis.

Steve looked at each item briefly before returning them to the envelope.

"We'll come back to those," he said. "Let me ask you a few questions. When you answer, please be as thorough as possible; no detail is too small."

"I'll tell you everything I can."

"Good," he said. "Naturally, I have to ask you where you were the night of the murder."

A look of *oh, no, not you too,* flashed across her face, but she moved past it.

"I was at a Zumba class, at the health club on Flagler Avenue. There were twenty people there who saw me. I didn't kill him," she said.

Steve wrote it down.

Okay," he said, "now let's start with the obvious. Can you think of anybody who would have wanted your husband dead?"

"I don't..." she shook her head, "...honestly, no. To be honest, Fred wasn't the most popular man in town. He could be arrogant and a bit of a loud-mouth. He had a tendency to annoy people, but I can't imagine somebody killing him for it."

"So, if you had to list people who might wish him harm, who would be the first five you could think of?"

Rhonda thought about it briefly and snickered slightly.

"Like I said, he had a way of getting under people's skin."

Steve looked at the attractive, and seemingly personable, woman across the desk and again asked himself how guys like Cranston did it. She could use whatever euphemism she liked, but Fred Cranston was an obnoxious jerk. It had taken Steve less than a week to figure that out.

"He talked about one of the sub-contractors on the hospital project all the time," she continued. "They seemed to butt heads quite a bit."

"Do you know his name?"

"His first name was Rick, his last name was something long and Italian—I can't remember it off-hand, but it reminded me of Capistrano."

Steve made a note.

"Who else?"

"Well, he liked to gamble, maybe he owed lots of money."

"Okay, that's good," he said, making a note to talk to Ralph Donabedian, the area's biggest bookie.

"A few weeks ago he had an argument with a man named Roger Thornton."

"What was the argument about?"

"Fred coached a girls' softball team, Roger complained constantly about his daughter not playing enough. He blamed Fred for her not getting a scholarship. One morning Fred left for work and his car tires were all flat. He swore up and down Thornton was behind it."

Steve continued writing.

"Anyone else?"

"Well…"

"Anything you can think of," Steve encouraged.

"Well, it's a little strange, but…" she hesitated, "one of our neighbors had a dog. It was a little Chihuahua—Fred hated it because it would come into our yard and dig holes or poop on the lawn. Sometimes it would bark at night."

"Did he have words with the neighbor?"

"Worse," she said. "The dog went missing last month. The neighbor, Mr. Pezullo, accused Fred of doing something to the dog. They exchanged words several times."

"Did Fred do something to the dog?"

"If he did, he never said anything to me about it."

"Where does Mr. Pezullo live?"

"Number 73, diagonally across the street from us."

"Okay, now tell me about his personal habits," Steve said. "Did he play golf? Was he a member of the Rotary? What did he do when he wasn't at home or work?"

"He did play golf, usually on Sunday with some men from work," she said, "Brian, Tony and Juan are their names, I don't know their last names. They would usually make a day of it. He coached the softball team and once in a while he played poker in Daytona. Other than that he worked a lot, attended conferences, or at least that's what I used to think until I found out about his girlfriend."

Steve made a final note on the pad and moved it aside.

"I think I have enough to get started," Steve said. "If I think of anything else, I'll call you."

Steve walked her to the door and watched her drive off, still wondering about her motive for trying to solve her husband's murder.

~*THREE*~

Steve returned to his desk and dialed the phone.

"Detective Ray Gallucci, please," he said when his call was answered.

"This is Detective Gallucci," a voice picked up.

"Hello, detective, this is Steve Salem, we met last night."

"Right, right," Gallucci said, "the homicide at the bar on Nova Road. What can I do for you?"

"I was wondering if you've identified the female victim yet."

Steve heard some paper being shuffled before Gallucci answered.

"Yes, victim has been identified as 24-year-old Charlotte June Miller, aka CJ Miller. She was a dancer at The Meat Locker, on Clyde Morris Boulevard, went by the name Eve Adams."

"Ahh," Steve said, "a *religious* girl."

"Everybody's looking for a new angle," Gallucci said. "From what I hear, she danced with a snake."

"Wouldn't it be a serpent, then?"

"Yeah," the detective said, "as it were."

"Can you give me an address and a date of birth on her?" Steve asked.

He wrote the information on his pad, thanked Gallucci and hung up, then immediately placed another call.

"Computer Information Associates," a voice answered in a near-whisper. "Bill Eldredge speaking."

"Bill, it's Steve Salem."

"The witch hunter," Bill answered. "What can I do for you?"

"Are you busy?"

"Define busy."

"I need a couple of searches."

"Do you want the usual parameters?"

"Yeah, the full monty."

"I can have it for you in twenty-four hours, is that okay?"

"That'll be fine."

"All right, give me the names."

"Fred Cranston, 72 Pickering Lane, Palm Coast. Date of birth 29 July, 1966."

"And…"

"Charlotte June Miller, 804 Deen Road, Bunnell. Date of birth, 13 June, 1987.

Steve heard Bill typing the information—the computer whiz never used a pencil—and envisioned him sitting at his desk, in his immaculate home office—dressed like a banker with not a single hair out of place. Bill not only broke every stereotype of a computer geek, he shattered them.

"Anything else?"

"Just one thing," Steve said. "Cranston coached a girls' softball team, I'm assuming in Flagler County, see if you can find out which league, and a roster of the girls on his team would help."

"That shouldn't be a problem," Bill said.

"Thanks, Bill."

"I'll call you tomorrow," Bill said.

Steve stepped into his flip-flops and left the office.

It was a bit early in the day to look for Ralph Donabedian so he decided to start by talking to Rhonda's neighbor—the one with the missing dog.

Twenty minutes later he pulled to the side of the road in front of a pastel-salmon colored house with a four-foot high, plastic dolphin for a mailbox. It was an average Florida home, approximately 2500-square feet, with an attached garage. In the driveway was a burgundy Mercury Sable, the sister car to the Ford Taurus.

Steve suddenly wished he had brought his gun.

He rang the doorbell and, after a few seconds, saw veiled movement through the opaque, oval-shaped window in the door.

His concerns about being unarmed subsided when the door opened to reveal a bent old man. A small oxygen tank hung around his shoulder and two clear plastic tubes ran from it to his nose. His hair was snow-white and his complexion was pasty, at best. When he spoke his hoarse voice sounded out of breath.

"I ain't buying, especially if you're pushing God," he said before Steve could speak.

Steve held his hands up.

"That's okay," he said, "I'm not selling anything."

The old man looked at him quizzically.

"Whaddya want?"

"I'm looking for Mr. Pezullo, are you he?"

"Who's asking?"

"My name is Steve Salem, I'm a private investigator."

The man raised his left eyebrow.

"What do you want with me?"

"Are you Mr. Pezullo?"

"Yeah."

"Can I talk to you about your neighbor, Fred Cranston."

"That jerk, I got nothing to say about him, he killed Chico."

"Chico?"

"My dog. Cranston was always complaining about Chico going in his yard, he hated Chico. Then one night Chico doesn't come when I call him…"

Pezullo choked up and had to fight tears.

"Why don't you investigate *that*?" the old man said.

"Can you think of anybody who might want to harm Mr. Cranston?"

"Anybody with an ounce of sense. Why do you want to know?"

Steve glanced at the car in the driveway, ignoring the man's question.

"Do you live alone, Mr. Pezullo?"

"I do now," he said. "Used to have Chico."

"Is that your car?"

"Yeah, of course it's my car. Whose car do you think it is? You don't think I can drive?"

"Not at all. Tell me, have you noticed anything unusual in the neighborhood recently?"

"Like what?"

"Anything different. Strange cars driving by, people you don't recognize."

"I keep to myself, got no truck with anybody."

"I understand," Steve said. "Thank you for your time, sir."

"You let me know if you find out what happened to Chico," Pezullo ordered.

"I will," Steve said as he turned and walked to his Jeep.

Before getting into the car, Steve looked across the street at the Cranston's home and decided to have a look around. Rhonda wasn't home, but he could check the outside.

The lawn looked as if it hadn't been mowed in a week or so, it was probably on Fred Cranston's final *to-do* list. A circular driveway dominated the front yard with a flagpole set in the grass at the top of the arch. The flag hung lifelessly in the stillness of the day. A small ceramic cat clung to the wall to the right of the front door.

The landscaping beds in front of the windows showed no sign of disturbance. When he turned the corner to the right side of the house he nearly walked into a garden hose wrapped on a wall-mounted rack. Other than the hose and the electric meter, there was nothing on the entire façade, least of all windows. At the back corner he checked the screen door of the pool enclosure. The handle was broken and the door opened.

The pool deck contained the usual patio furniture, barbeque grill, cooler and pool-associated items. One of the chairs at the glass-top table was out of place, other than that there didn't seem to be anything amiss.

He exited the enclosure through the door at the other side and walked past the filter, pump and Jacuzzi equipment. Spotting some footprints in the dirt below a window, he knelt down for a closer look. As he did, the pool filter kicked on, startling him slightly. Although the footprints disappeared into the surrounding grass, it certainly looked as if someone had approached from the street, stopped at the window and went back the way they had come. Thanks to the rain from the night before it was impossible to determine what size foot or what type of shoe had left the prints.

Halfway to the street he spotted a green, disposable, butane lighter in the grass. He picked it up carefully to avoid ruining any fingerprints and dropped it into his pocket. Bill Eldredge had, among other high-tech gadgets, a mobile fingerprint scanner with links to the national law enforcement database.

A window in the house next door—ten feet to his left—went up. Steve looked at the open window, thought about the lighter and the footprints, and walked to the front door of the house.

A rugged man in his early-thirties opened the door when Steve rang the bell.

"Hi," he said, searching Steve's face for recognition.

Steve offered his hand.

"Good morning, my name is Steve Salem, I'm a private investigator. Do you have a minute?"

The man shook Steve's hand.

"Sure," he said. "I'm Terry Aimes, what can I do for you?"

"I'd like to talk to you about your neighbor, Fred Cranston."

"Fred? What about him?"

"How well do you know him?"

"Not very, enough to say hi, stuff like that."

Steve nodded.

"When was the last time you saw him?"

Suspicion sprouted on Aimes' face.

"You got any kind of ID?" he asked.

Steve produced his Private Investigator's identification, Terry examined it and handed it back, satisfied.

"I guess the last time I saw him was, I don't know, Tuesday morning. I was leaving for work, he was too. I said '*Hey*', he waved and we drove off in opposite directions."

"Seen anything unusual lately? Strange cars, people you don't know?"

Aimes started to shake his head, then stopped.

"Actually, one day last week, Wednesday, I had a doctor's appointment, I came home from work early and there was a blue car in front of their house. It took off when I came around the corner. I thought it was funny since they're never home during the day."

"What kind of car?"

"I don't know, I suck at cars. Ask me about grass, that I know—I'm a landscaper."

"Did you see the driver?"

"I wasn't really paying attention, plus it had tinted windows."

"How about a license plate?"

"I do remember noticing that it wasn't a Florida plate, I know pretty much all of our different plates and it wasn't one of them. All I remember is it had mountains on it."

"You leave your windows open much?"

"Sure, this time of year, nice to get fresh air in the house."

"Have you ever noticed anything on the side, between your house and the Cranston's?"

"No, the rooms on that end of the house are just spare bedrooms, I hardly go in them."

Steve thought for a minute and was about to leave when he thought of one last question.

"How about Mr. Pezullo's dog?"

"Chico? He's a cool little dog, what about him."

"Seen him lately?"

Aimes looked up and thought.

"Now that you mention it, no. Not in a couple weeks, probably. I do remember hearing him barking like crazy one night, but that's about it."

"Do you know what night it was."

He shook his head slowly as he thought.

"No, no idea, sorry."

Steve handed him a business card.

"Thanks, Terry, you've been very helpful."

"Hey, what's this about?" Terry said, stopping Steve after a couple of steps. "Is everything okay? Did Fred do something wrong?"

"I'm afraid I can't answer that, I have an obligation to my client."

Steve walked to his Jeep before Terry could ask any more questions. In his Jeep, he took a small notebook from the glove box and recorded the highlights of the conversation.

~FOUR~

On his way back to Flagler Beach, Steve stopped at Rhonda Cranston's health club, a medium-sized metal building three blocks west of A1A, surrounded by a neighborhood of mobile homes.

There were only two cars in the lot when Steve walked to the door, a Mazda Miata and a Honda Civic, neither of which could be mistaken for a Ford Taurus.

He walked through the empty lobby into the carpeted workout space. It was a typical, low-budget gym, lacking in the amenities of the larger, corporate *personal fitness centers*. The mirrored walls made the space look larger than it was. The equipment was far from state-of-the-art and there were no good-looking, muscular kids walking around with smiles and matching, embroidered polo shirts. The only person in sight was a muscular man in shorts and a tank top jumping rope in the corner.

"Excuse me," Steve said, approaching the man.

The man stopped jumping abruptly and turned.

"Oh, hey, I didn't hear you come in," he said. "We don't open for another hour."

"That's okay," Steve said, "I'm not here to work out."

The man hung his jump-rope over a rack of barbells.

"What can I do for you?"

Steve handed him a business card.

"My name is Steve Salem, I'm a private investigator. Can I ask you a couple of questions?"

The man scrutinized the card and handed it back to Steve.

"What about?" he said.

"What was your name?" Steve asked.

"Chris, Chris Tucker."

"Are you the manager?"

"Owner, manager, janitor, you name it."

"Do you have a member here by the name of Rhonda Cranston?"

Tucker's flinch was barely noticeable, but Steve saw it.

"Rhonda Cranston? Uhh, I don't know off the top of my head. Why?"

"Can you check? It's important."

With a skeptical eye at Steve, Tucker walked toward a small office. Steve followed, thankful that the general public was largely unaware of their option to tell private investigators to take a hike.

Inside the small office, a petite woman wearing workout clothing and far too much makeup sat behind a computer holding a pencil in her right hand and quickly punching calculator keys with her left.

"Grace," Tucker said to her, "this man is a private investigator; he needs some information on a member,"

Grace looked at Steve and smiled.

"Hi, who is the member?"

"Rhonda Cranston."

The name struck a chord with her, which she attempted to mask with another smile, but it didn't escape Steve.

"What about her?" Grace said to Steve, her smile gone.

"Is she a member here?"

"Yes, she is," Grace said, with a look at Tucker. "He didn't tell you?"

"No," Steve said, noticing Tucker squirming slightly.

Hanging on the wall behind her, Steve spotted a photo of Chris and Grace, together on a cruise ship. He glanced briefly at the wedding band on her finger.

"What do want to know about her?" Grace asked.

"Was she here last night?"

Grace looked at Tucker before answering.

"Yes, she was. Zumba class, 7:00-8:00."

"Did she get here early, stay late?"

"She probably arrived around 6:45 and I believe she left at about 8:15."

"Was there anything unusual about her behavior?"

"Unusual, how?"

"Anything different. Did she argue with anyone? Was there somebody waiting for her in the parking lot? Did she seem anxious or nervous?"

"No," Grace said. "Nothing I can think of, but I'm not here to monitor people's behavior."

"Okay," Steve said, "that's really all I needed to know."

Grace popped out of her chair, sending it rolling backward into the wall.

"If you'll excuse me," she said, and walked out of the office.

"Something I said?" Steve asked after she was gone.

"Women," Tucker said, aiming for a sympathetic *guy* moment.

"How long have you two been married?"

"Eight years, almost."

"I take it she doesn't care much for Rhonda Cranston."

"Like I said…" he shrugged "…women."

Steve looked at him silently for several seconds hoping to elicit more information, but Tucker said nothing, just made an exaggerated effort of examining one of his fingernails.

"Were you teaching the class last night?" Steve asked.

"No, Grace ran last night's class, I wasn't here. What's this all about?"

"I'm sorry, I can't answer that. Mind telling me where you were?"

Tucker dropped the guy bonding thing and furrowed his brow.

"I'm sorry," he mimicked, "I can't answer that."

"I see," Steve said, making a mental note to look into Chris Tucker a little further.

Steve dropped his card on the desk and looked at Tucker.

"I'll leave that in case you think of anything else you want to tell me."

"Right," Tucker said.

Steve turned off A1A into the small gravel parking lot next to a restaurant called The Golden Lion. A white fence surrounded a courtyard with covered outdoor seating, a bandstand/gazebo and a tiki bar.

He walked to an outdoor table in the corner by the stairs. Seated at the table were a man in a wheelchair and another man the size of a professional wrestler.

"Hi, Ralphy," Steve said to the man in the wheelchair, then to the other man, "Ike."

Ralph Donabedian looked up from his wheelchair.

"Steve Salem, as I live and breathe," he said. "Look Ike, it's everybody's favorite P.I."

Ike nodded a hello to Steve.

"Mind if I sit down for a minute?" Steve asked.

"Not at all," Ralph said. "Can I buy you a drink?"

"No thanks, I just wanted to ask you a couple of questions."

"Shoot," Ralph said.

"You know a guy named Fred Cranston?"

"I do."

"What can you tell me about him?"

"Aside from the fact that he's dead?"

"Well, good news certainly travels fast," Steve said. "Yeah, aside from that."

"Is this conversation off the record?"

"Did you kill him?"

"Absolutely not."

"Then we're off the record."

"Okay," Ralph took a sip of clear liquid from his glass. "Fred was a betting man."

"One of your regulars?"

"Not any more. I stopped taking his action last year. He had a bad habit of betting over his head. I had to send Ike to...*talk to him*...too many times," Ralph said with a nod at his companion.

"Would you say he had a gambling problem?"

"A problem?" Ralph said with an ironic laugh. "Losing your car keys is a problem—Cranston had an addiction."

"Who'd he bet with after you dropped him?"

"He went to a minor league jerk in Bunnell."

"You know his name?"

"What's that punk's name, Ike?" Ralph said. "Jeff, John...?"

"Santoro," Ike answered, "John Santoro."

"That's him," Ralph said. "I call him Jabba the Mutt, pudgy little stain thinks he's tough."

"You wouldn't happen to know if Cranston was in deep with him, would you?"

"I wouldn't doubt it," Ralph said, "and Santoro's just stupid enough to kill him for it."

"Stupid enough?" Steve asked.

"Yeah, stupid. Dead men don't pay their debts, but a maggot like Santoro doesn't think like that, he's got the IQ of a brick. That's why he'll never make it to the bigs. He's so low on the radar he couldn't get arrested if he tried."

Steve nodded.

"Know where I can find him?"

"He usually hangs out at a dive in Bunnell called Rebs."

"I know it," Steve said. "Thanks for your time, Ralph."

Steve stood and shook the hands of both men.

"Take care," he said.

~FIVE~

Back in his office, Steve examined the contents of the envelope Rhonda had given him.

He started with the bank statements. After thirty minutes he had found only one transaction that seemed worthy of scrutiny. A cash withdrawal, made three weeks before Fred's death, in the amount of $1,800.

The day-planner was fairly cluttered with appointments, meetings, phone numbers and doodles, but nothing leapt off the page as suspicious. At this point in the investigation he was still working to establish a pattern of behavior in order to have a basis for comparison. When he flipped to the date corresponding to the cash withdrawal on the bank statement there was a notation:

***$$$ - ACE 2:30*.**

Steve made a note to ask Rhonda what light, if any, she could shed on it.

Also of interest were several three-day clusters, one or two per month, blocked out with the notation *seminar* in bold letters. Bill should be able to verify that easily enough.

According to the college reunion invitation, Fred had attended the University of Florida and majored in Building Construction, graduating in 1988. The reunion had taken place two weeks ago. It was too late to follow up on it, but he could ask Rhonda if Fred had attended.

The credit card statement was much too clean for Steve's liking. All of the charges were completely predictable; gas stations, restaurants, and an occasional purchase at a department store.

"This is obviously the credit card you wanted your wife to see, Fred," Steve said. "Nobody is this squeaky-clean."

Another item for Bill to confirm.

Holding Cranston's cell phone bill, Steve picked up his phone and dialed the most frequently called number. The call went straight to voice mail and Steve listened to the sound of a girl in her early twenties...

"Hi, it's CJ. I know you're dying to talk to me but I'm doing something else at the moment. (coy laugh) *Leave me a message and when I'm done with what I'm doing I'll think about calling you!"*

He hung up and looked at the list of calls. He recognized the second most frequently called number as Rhonda's. Dialing the next number in line he got the answering service for Fred's employer.

"Hello, you've reached the offices of Halsey-Taylor Construction, if you know your party's extension..."

He hung up.

Several more calls took him to fast-food joints, building supply stores, the offices of various subcontractors and his auto mechanic.

The next number Steve dialed had been called by Fred Cranston every Wednesday and Friday, at various times between 2:30 and 4:00.

"Yeah," a gruff, male voice answered.

"Fred Cranston?" Steve said.

"What about him?"

"Is he there?"

"Who's this?"

"A friend."

"You got the wrong fuckin' number, friend," the voice said before hanging up.

Steve went to his computer and did a reverse lookup of the number, the listing came back as *Unlisted Cell Phone – Bunnell, Florida.*

"Mr. Santoro, I assume," Steve said, making a note of the number.

Of all the numbers on the list, there was one that stood out for its infrequency. It was an incoming call, two days before Cranston's murder. Steve dialed the number. The call was answered by a male voice thick with sleep.

"Hello."

"Hey, did I wake you up?" Steve asked.

"Yeah, what's up?"

"What's going on?"

There was a brief pause.

"Who's this?"

"Is that you, Billy?" Steve asked.

"No it ain't Billy," the voice said with irritation, "who's this?"

"It's Fred Cranston."

The line went dead immediately—back to reverse lookup. *Unlisted Landline-Flagler Beach, Florida.*

Steve called Bill Eldredge.

"Computer Information Associates, Bill Eldredge speaking."

"Hi, Bill, it's Steve."

"Steve, I don't have anything for you yet."

"I know, Bill, I was wondering if you could do a quick phone number search for me, I don't have your powers of access."

Steve heard the clicking of a keyboard.

"What's the number?"

"386-555-4205"

More keyboard clicks followed by a short pause.

"Okay, the number is listed to a Brian Townsend, South Seventh Street, Flagler Beach. If I'm not mistaken it's in the trailer park just south of the police station."

"I think you're right, Bill. Can you add Townsend to the list for tomorrow?"

"Sure, I'll see what I can find."

"And one more thing…"

"Yes?"

"I think Fred Cranston may have had a credit card his wife didn't know about."

"If he did, I'll find it."

"Thanks, Bill."

Steve hung up and wrote the information down.

Last in the pile were the three photographs. The first showed Fred, fifty pounds ago, on a beach with Rhonda. Rhonda was lying in the standard sunbathing position, while Fred sat in a sand chair with a copy of Sports Illustrated in one hand and a beer in the other. On the back of the picture was written *"Cabo - 2004"*

The next was a picture of Fred and three other men on a golf course. One of the men wore a polo shirt with the familiar logo of Halsey-Taylor on the left breast. Since there was no writing on the back, Steve assumed these were Fred's work/golf buddies.

In the third picture, which was much older, four people in their early twenties were captured in a moment of youthful exuberance. There were three men and a woman, and judging by the haircuts and clothing it had been taken in the mid-eighties. Steve recognized the man on the far right as a younger Fred Cranston. To Fred's right was a tall thin guy with a cigar in his mouth. Next to him was a young girl, slightly taller than average with blonde hair and a pretty *girl next door* look. The young man on the far left had his arm around the girl. He was approximately the same height and weight as Cranston with similar features.

Faded ink on the back said *Fred, Brenda, Paul, Walt.* There was no date or location but on closer examination Steve spotted the famous fountain of Las Vegas' Bellagio hotel in the background. The picture was, for all intents and purposes, worthless to Steve at this point.

After over an hour of sitting at the desk, Steve's back was getting stiff. He stood, stretched and walked to the kitchen for a beer. He went to the front porch for a look at the ocean across the street. It was a quiet afternoon and the sea was calm. A few people rode bicycles along A1A and traffic was sparse. Looking south, he noticed a car parked on the shoulder two blocks away—it was similar in size and shape to a Ford Taurus. Shielding his eyes with his hand he tried to get a better look but he couldn't make out any detail or see if it was occupied.

Squelching his reflexive suspicion, he allowed his thoughts to turn to Fred Cranston.

A man with a decent job, beautiful wife and a nice home, many would say he had it all. Fred didn't seem to see it that way, though. Fred seemed to want something more—or something different anyway.

Steve had seen lots of *Fred Cranstons* over the years, and had yet to figure out what it is that makes people want whatever it is they don't have.

Once, on a boring day of driving a patrol car in Boston, Steve and his partner had a conversation about it.

"Why do they do it, Hink?" Steve asked Todd Hinkley, his partner.

"Do what?" Hinkley asked as he lowered his sunglasses to check out a pack of co-eds walking through Kenmore Square.

"Why is it that no matter how good people have it, they always want more? Why can't we ever be satisfied with what we have?"

"Maybe it's not in our DNA."

"You mean, no matter what we have, we'll always want something else?"

"Could be, it seems to be the predominant pattern."

"So there's no solution? That what you're saying?"

"Not one that I know of, this is like the chicken or the egg…the tree falling in the forest, that kind of stuff. If I knew the answer I wouldn't be riding in this car right now."

They rode in silence for several minutes.

"Of course," Hinkley said, "if I did find the answer, I wouldn't like it and I'd try to learn more. That's human nature, man. Ever since we invented the wheel we've been trying to come up with ways to make it go faster."

"So you think we should consider everything we have as being temporary? Jobs, money, knowledge, relationships?"

"Especially relationships, as far as I'm concerned, they're the most temporary thing there is."

Steve often missed Hinkley's ability to get to the essence of a conversation. He was not a man who would ever be accused of over-thinking anything, which sometimes gave him an advantage in understanding people. It was a trait Steve still tried to emulate.

He glanced south again and the car was gone. He wondered if it was something to be concerned about, after all, it was possible the shooter in the Taurus had seen him.

Or maybe he was over-thinking again.

Putting the mystery car out of his mind, Steve went back to his desk and called Rhonda Cranston.

"I'm sorry to be so blunt," he said, "but I need to know if there's something going on between you and Chris Tucker, from the gym."

"God, no," the exasperation obvious in her voice, "I can't stand that egotistical jerk—if he comes on to me one more time I'm going straight to his wife."

"So you're saying he tried to initiate something with you?"

"He's constantly trying, but I keep telling him we're both married and he should have a little more respect. At first I tried to be polite, but lately I've had to get rude with him. I'm afraid to imagine what he'll be like when he finds out about Fred."

"Did he know Fred?"

"Not personally, no...at least not that I know of."

"How does he usually react when you reject him?"

"He's not happy, but he looks at me like he's thinking *'It's only a matter of time before you say yes'*. Then he'll go and hit on another woman, all while his wife is fifty feet away."

"Is he ever overly aggressive?"

She considered the question for a moment.

"I don't know if I'd call it aggressive," she said. "I'd say it was more like persistent."

"I understand," he said.

Certainly explains his wife's attitude problem, Steve thought.

"Rhonda, can you tell me anything about an eighteen-hundred dollar cash withdrawal from your bank account last month?"

"Eighteen-hundred?" she said. "I have no idea what that would have been for."

Gambling debt, Steve assumed.

"Does the name John Santoro mean anything to you?"

"Nothing," she said. "Who is that?"

"I'm not sure yet," Steve said, "probably nobody. How about Brian Townsend?"

"No, I've never heard that name either."

"Do you know anybody called Ace or maybe with the initials A.C.E.?"

"No, I'm sorry."

So Fred's mistress wasn't the only secret he was keeping, Steve thought.

"I'd like to ask you about the pictures you left with me."

"Okay."

"In the picture of Fred and his golf buddies, can you tell me the names of the other men and anything you know about them."

"Oh, sure," she said. "The black man is Juan Bostwick, he's an engineer on the hospital project Fred is...*was* working on."

She paused briefly.

"I'm sorry," she said, "I'm still adjusting to speaking about him in the past tense."

"Perfectly understandable," Steve said. "Did Fred ever mention any issues with him?"

"With Juan? Heavens, no. Fred and Juan got along very well."

"Okay, how about the others."

"The man with the shaved head is Brian Chamberlain, he's a project manager at Halsey-Taylor. Fred never had any problems with him either. The other man is Tony Capela, he's Fred's right-hand-man at H-T." she paused briefly, "I guess he'll be next in line for Fred's position."

People have certainly killed for much less things than a high-paying job, Steve thought, making a note to look into the golf buddies, but it didn't seem like a high priority.

"What was Fred's title?"

"Vice President of Operations."

"And this other picture, the old one," Steve said. "I assume it's Fred and some friends, back in the day."

"Right," she said. "That's one of the only pictures Fred has from his past. It was taken when he was in college. He was adopted as a child and his adoptive parents died when their house burned down. All of his childhood memories were destroyed in the fire."

"Do you know anything about the people in the picture with him?"

"Not really, he didn't talk about his past very much. I think he once mentioned that one of the other men in the picture was killed."

"Do you know which one?"

"No."

"Did he say it like that, 'he was killed', or did he just say 'he was dead'?"

"I don't remember, I never really gave it any thought."

"So you can't remember if Fred told you how he died?"

"No, I'm sorry."

Steve looked over his notes, "Oh, just out of curiosity, did Fred attend his college reunion?"

"No, he missed it, he had to go away on business that weekend."

Business in Vegas, Steve thought.

"Okay, that does it for now, sorry to keep bothering you like this, but I like to ask questions before I forget."

"No apology necessary, I'm sorry I wasn't very helpful," she said."

"You did fine," Steve said, "one more thing."

"Yes?"

"I don't want you to be alarmed, but…"

"But what?"

"I think it would be a good idea for you to start being aware of your surroundings, keep an eye out for cars that seem to be following you, strangers in the neighborhood, things like that."

"Why, is there somebody after *me* now?"

"I doubt it, but if you see anything unusual, anything at all, call me immediately, whatever time it is."

"Okay," she said nervously. "I will. Is there anything else?"

"I don't think so,"

Steve hung up and put the items back into the envelope.

~SEVEN~

Steve's slow-moving Sunday morning was interrupted by his cell phone. The display showed the name *Leonard Kleinrock*. With a knowing grin, he answered the call.

"Good morning, Bill," he said. "Still using the Kleinrock alias, I see."

"It's not an alias," Bill Eldredge replied, "it's a tribute. You've got Sam Spade, I've got Leonard Kleinrock."

"Fair enough," Steve said. "What's up?

"I've got your information, when can we meet?"

"How about I buy you lunch? Golden Lion, 12:00?"

"That's fine, I'll see you there."

"Bill, one more thing."

"What's that?"

"Can you bring your mobile fingerprint kit?"

"No problem."

At noon Steve parked on the shoulder of A1A and entered the courtyard of The Golden Lion.

Ralph Donabedian and Ike sat at their usual table—he stopped on his way to the stairs.

"Hey, guys," he said.

"Steve Salem," Ralph said. "Do we know who killed Fred yet?"

"Not yet, but I'm working on it."

Steve walked up the stairs and took a seat along the rail on the upper deck.

Before the waitress returned with his beer, Bill Eldredge arrived carrying a manila folder and small, black, nylon case.

"I love this view," Bill said as he sat.

"Doesn't get much better," Steve agreed, "especially since they expanded."

Bill placed the case and the folder on the table between them.

"You need some fingerprint work?" Bill said as he opened the case.

"Yeah," Steve said, removing a plastic sandwich bag from his pocket. From the bag he withdrew the cigarette lighter from Rhonda Cranston's yard and handed it to Bill.

Using a soft-bristled brush Bill applied black powder to the lighter, then examined it.

"Looks like we have a couple of usable prints," he said.

He placed a piece of clear plastic film over a print, carefully removed it and placed it on the display screen of a hand-held device resembling something the crew of the Starship Enterprise would carry.

He pushed a couple of buttons and set the device aside.

"That'll probably take a few minutes," he said. "If the person who used that lighter has ever been fingerprinted, we'll know shortly."

"So what else do you have?" Steve asked.

Bill opened the file folder.

"First, here's the information on Cranston's involvement with the Flagler County Girls' Softball League, including his team roster."

Steve flipped through the pages quickly and placed it on the table. Although some parents did tend to get a little over zealous at their children's sporting events, Steve wasn't prepared to suspect one of murder…yet.

"Next."

"You were right," Bill said, pulling more pages from the folder. "Cranston had another credit card he kept hidden from his wife. The statements were sent to Miss Miller's house and she's listed as an authorized user on the account."

"Nice," Steve said.

"Lots of charges for women's clothing, adult novelty stores and expensive restaurants, but there's something else. Cranston was going to Vegas at least once a month, sometimes twice."

"I've heard he liked to gamble," Steve said. "He told his wife he was going to work-related seminars."

"Nice work, if you can get it," Bill said.

"Yeah," Steve agreed, "what else?"

"First of all, you gave me the wrong birthday for him," Bill said. "You told me 29 July, 1966, according to the Bureau of Statistics, he was actually born on 17 September, 1967."

"Really? That's the date his wife gave me, she was pretty emotional at the time so she probably gave me their anniversary or something. I'll double-check with her, I trust it didn't impede your search."

Eldredge grinned.

"Frederick David Cranston, born—as we now know—September 17, 1967 to a seventeen-year-old girl from North Carolina named Melissa Joan Cote. He was put up for adoption almost immediately. He was adopted by Arthur and Emily Cranston of Jacksonville, Florida."

"I'm not going to ask how you got that information," Steve interrupted, "it's supposed to be highly confidential."

Bill wiggled his eyebrows, "If it's on a computer, the term *highly confidential* is nothing more than a speed bump."

"Good to know," Steve said.

"Back to Fred Cranston," Bill continued, "no problems as a kid, good grades, worked his way through college as a caretaker in a cemetery. Attended the University of Florida, Bachelor's Degree in Building Construction, Deans List, no disciplinary action. During his sophomore year, his parents' home was destroyed in a fire, they were both killed. Nothing suspicious about the fire, it was ruled accidental and blamed on an overloaded extension cord in the garage. Cranston finished school and graduated in 1988."

Bill paused when a waitress appeared—after she left with their order he resumed his briefing.

"Before being hired by Halsey-Taylor Construction as an estimator in 1990, he worked for a company called Emerson Home Builders in Ocala. He moved up the ranks at Halsey-Taylor steadily until he was named VP of Operations in 2004. His reported income last year was $178,000. No dependents, no military service, no criminal record, one D.U.I in 2006. He married Rhonda Marie L'Heureux in 2001."

"So what you're telling me is that, other than his involvement with CJ Miller, he's lived a quiet, normal life?"

"Not necessarily," Bill said. "I'm telling you he lived below the radar. I can find a lot of information, but only if it's in a computer somewhere."

"So if it's not in the grid, you can't find it."

"Exactly, if he got caught smoking in the boys room, it'll be invisible to me unless it's in a computer somewhere. If he was in a bar-room brawl, I can't find it unless a police report was filed. If he had a car accident, I won't know unless a police report was filed or an insurance claim was submitted."

"Gotcha," Steve said.

"Point of interest," Bill added with a grin, "Cranston was sterile."

"Sterile? As in couldn't have children?"

"Yes sir. His batteries weren't fully charged."

"Hardly seems relevant, but thanks for the heads up," Steve said.

At this point, it was looking as though Fred's involvement with CJ Miller and/or his propensity for gambling had been the key factors in his downfall.

"Is that it?"

"Those are the highlights for Cranston," Bill said. "I'll let you look through the rest. Let's move on to Miss Miller."

"Let's do."

At that moment Bill's fingerprint device let out three beeps.

"Uh-oh," Bill said, "I think we have something."

He picked up the device and shielded the screen from the sun.

"Okay," he said, "the winner is...Dean Ericson, born 18 November, 1982. Mr. Ericson is currently on parole after serving four years out of a six year sentence for aggravated assault and assault with a dangerous weapon."

"Any specifics on the charges?" Steve asked.

"Not on this device, just his rap sheet. Last known address is in Palatka," Bill wrote the address on the manila folder. "When I get home I can do a complete check on him if you'd like."

"Yeah, if you have the time, that'd be good." Steve said.

"Moving right along," Bill said. "On to Charlotte June Miller—you had her birthday correct, 13 June, 1987—she grew up in Port Angeles, Washington, moved to Florence, South Carolina in 2000. In 2001 she was raped by one of her middle school teachers. The case was thrown out of court on a technicality, something about the chain of evidence. She never finished school, dropped out in the tenth grade. In 2005 she moved to Daytona Beach. She's been arrested three times for prostitution and was currently on probation. Her employer is listed as Wooden Member Entertainment, I take it you know they own a number of *gentleman's clubs* in central Florida."

"Yeah, she worked hard for the money," Steve said.

"The last time she was arrested was about a month ago. Her bail was posted by Ace Bonds, but you'll never guess who the indeminitor was."
"Fred Cranston?"

Bill touched his nose and pointed at Steve.

"On the nosey," he said.

"And the bail amount was set at $18,000, right?"

"Right again. How'd you know?"

"Fred made a cash withdrawal for $1,800 I couldn't account for."

"Ten percent," Bill nodded. "Mystery solved."

"One, anyway," Steve said. "Anything else?"

"There is one other interesting item. Charlotte filed a restraining order shortly after she was bailed out."

"Don't tell me it was against Cranston."

"No, it was against Brian Townsend."

It took Steve a second to recall the name.

"No kidding?"

"Strike me dead," Bill said, raising his right hand.

"So we have a connection."

"It would appear so," Bill said. "And speaking of Mr. Townsend..."

"Please, enlighten me," Steve said.

"Brian William Townsend, born on April Fool's Day, 1983 in New York city—the Bronx to be specific. His father is currently serving life for multiple homicides and his mother is on parole for a variety of drug and prostitution related charges."

"I guess the turd doesn't fall far from the asshole," Steve interrupted.

Bill looked at him with a raised eyebrow.

"How eloquent," he said.

"I call 'em like I see 'em," Steve said. "Please continue."

"Townsend opted for reform school over high school. He was sent in when he was fourteen after he and a buddy were busted for home invasion. He was released on his twenty-first birthday and promptly moved to Florida. He lived in Miami for a couple of years before he moved north to Flagler Beach. He's been arrested on a handful of drug charges and once for conspiracy in a prostitution sting. He doesn't have a valid driver's license, but he's got three D.U.I.s."

"Sounds like he's almost ready to run for office," Steve said.

Bill laughed and nodded.

"As I suspected," Bill went on, "he lives in the trailer park near the police station, I've printed you a Google map of the location."

"Bill, you never let me down," Steve said. "Send me a bill?"

"Already in the mail," Bill said, dropping his napkin onto his plate and standing. "Thanks for lunch."

They shook hands and Bill left. Steve paid for lunch, and walked to his car, carrying the folder of information.

~EIGHT~

On his way to the trailer-park home of Brian Townsend, Steve called Rhonda Cranston.

"Rhonda," he said, "does the name Dean Ericson mean anything to you?"

There was a brief silence before she answered.

"No," she said. "I'm sorry, I don't remember ever hearing that name."

"Okay, I just wanted to check. I'll be in touch."

Steve hung up and turned his Jeep into the parking lot of a US Post Office across the street from Townsend's trailer-park. Three high school kids were using the handicap ramp to perform skateboard tricks.

Across the street, four guys in their mid-twenties stood around a car while rap music blared from the open hatch-back. They were dressed in classic ghetto-garb…backward baseball hats, baggie shorts hanging low exposing plaid boxers, tank-tops or double-extra-large tee-shirts and high top sneakers.

"White, suburban homeboys," Steve snickered to himself as he crossed the street.

The homeboys stopped their conversation and turned to size-up the intruder. Steve continued past them, showing no concern for their watchdogging.

He followed the cracked and worn asphalt walkway between trailers past yards of dead grass, abandoned bicycles and the rotting carcasses of cars, boats and trucks.

In front of Townsend's trailer, an old Honda Prelude was parked in the front yard, it was hard to tell if it was drivable or not. In the reflection of the passenger's window Steve noticed two of the homeboys moving slowly along the walk in his direction.

After knocking on the dirty, aluminum storm-door, he took a step back and waited.

No response.

He knocked again, this time louder.

The inner door opened and a grizzled man in his mid-twenties stared at him through the rusty screen.

"Yeah?" the man said, rubbing sleep from his face.

"Brian Townsend?" Steve said.

The man scratched his crotch and scrutinized his visitor, then his eyes flicked to something behind Steve. Casually shifting his body position, Steve noticed the two homeboys were hanging out three doors down, failing miserably at looking casual.

"Who the fuck are you?" the man asked.

"Are you Brian?"

"I said 'Who the fuck *are* you', asshole."

"My name is Steve Salem, I'm a private investigator. Just have a couple of questions for you about a guy named Fred Cranston."

"Hang on," the man said after a brief pause, "lemmee put some pants on."

Steve took a step back and glanced at the homeboys, who were doing their best to look intimidating.

Steve heard the sound of the storm door crashing open and, before he could react, he was knocked to the ground by the fleeing man from the trailer. He jumped to his feet and ran after him.

The man ran toward the homeboys and they parted as if they were the Red Sea and the fleeing man was Moses.

The two kids stepped in front of Steve and one of them lifted his tank top to reveal a nine millimeter handgun tucked into the waistband of his boxers. Expecting Steve to stop in his tracks, they were taken by surprise when he lowered his shoulder and plowed the kid with the gun to the ground, knocking the air from his lungs. As the kid lay on the asphalt gasping for breath, Steve removed the gun from his boxers and brought it up to bear on the other one, who was moving toward him.

"Forget it," Steve said. "This doesn't concern you."

"The fuck it don't," the kid said, jutting his chin and raising his arm to point an imaginary glock, gangsta-style, at Steve. "You're a dead mother-fucker. Hear me?"

"Lift your shirt," Steve ordered.

The kid lifted his shirt and did a slow turn-around, no weapons.

"Lay down next to your boyfriend," Steve said, "arms and legs spread out."

The kid did as he was told.

"Stay there," Steve said as he resumed his chase.

The man he assumed was Townsend climbed into the car with the other two homeboys. The car peeled away, heading for State Road 100.

Steve raced past the three skateboarders and climbed into his Jeep. Jumping the curb, he took off after the car.

When he reached the light at Flagler Avenue and SR 100 there was no sign of them. If they had taken a left, Steve would still be able to see their car as it crossed the bridge over the intra-coastal waterway. The other two options were not so easy. Straight would take them into a grid of streets in a crowded neighborhood and right would take them to A1A a short distance away where they could go north or south and be out of sight in minutes.

Steve gave up the chase and picked up the folder Bill had given him. He entered the last known address of Dean Ericson into his portable GPS and followed the directions to Palatka.

He would pick up Brian Townsend's trail another time.

As he exited Interstate 95 onto State Road 207 his cell phone rang.

"Hello," he answered.

"Steve, it's Bill Eldredge, I've got something very interesting."

"What is it?"

"I was doing a little poking around, trying to find a connection between Townsend, Cranston and Miller and you won't believe what I found."

"I'm listening."

"I was looking at Townsend's Facebook page, of all things, and last week he posted an open hit on CJ Miller."

"On Facebook?"

"Believe it or not."

"Not very bright, is he? We can probably report it to the police, it should be enough for them to issue an arrest warrant."

"Not really," Bill said.

"Why not?"

"It's the way he worded it, I think it's vague enough to avoid legal action."

"What's it say?"

"He tagged a picture of her with the message *Somebody please take this bitch out,*" Bill said. "A first year law student would be able to fight it."

"Yeah, it isn't very specific, it could mean taking her out on a date as far as the law is concerned."

"Exactly."

"Were there any responses?"

"A few, but no serious takers. I'll send you a link."

"Bill, while you're working on it, could you see if you can find any connection between Townsend and Ericson?"

"Sure thing," Bill said. "I'll call you."

Steve put his phone away as the GPS unit told him to turn right. After a short drive through a crowded and much-forgotten main drag full of abandoned mills, video stores and used furniture warehouses, he entered a neighborhood of narrow streets and very old homes where property maintenance was not high on the list of priorities.

Steve drove past Ericson's house slowly. There was a motorcycle and a van in the driveway. The van was painted to look like sparkling, blue water. The words "Clearwater Pools" took up most of the side with a phone number and website address below it. There was also a car parked on the street in front of the house which was the same size and style as a Ford Taurus.

If Townsend and Ericson knew each other there was a good chance Ericson might be expecting trouble so Steve decided against direct contact. He drove past the house and turned into the driveway of a vacant home with a good view of Ericson's house.

Directory assistance connected him to Ericson's number and the call was answered on the third ring. Steve heard a television in the background, it sounded like Ericson was watching a football game.

"Yeah, hello" the call was answered by someone who was obviously not happy with the distraction.

"Is this Dean?" Steve asked.

Shouts of several voices went up in the background. Steve heard somebody yell "touchdown!"

"Damn it, I missed it," the voice on the phone said. "This is Dean, who's this?" he said to Steve.

"I'm calling about Brian Townsend."

"Who?" Ericson said. "Holy shit they missed the point?" he yelled to somebody else.

"Brian Townsend," Steve repeated.

"Who's that? Never heard of him."

"Sorry, wrong number," Steve said as he hung up then placed a call to Rhonda Cranston.

"Rhonda," he said, "do you use a pool cleaning service?"

"Yes, we do," she said. "Clearwater Pools, why?"

"Just checking," Steve said. "Do they always send the same person?"

"Yeah, pretty much, unless he's on vacation or something. I know his name, let me think," she said, "begins with a D - Don, Dave, something like that."

"What do you think of him?"

"Think of him? I don't know. He seems okay. Doesn't say much, he does good work, our pool is always spotless. I think the only thing I don't like about him are his tattoos, they're kind of…I don't know…mean looking."

Sounds like prison ink Steve thought.

"When's he scheduled to come back?"

"Not for another two weeks."

"Okay, that's all I need for now."

Steve started the Jeep and drove away. Ericson's lighter in the yard was easily explainable and without an obvious connection between him and Townsend Steve felt there was nothing to be gained from approaching him at this time.

~NINE~

Monday morning Rhonda Cranston called for a status update and Steve was reluctant to say much—not wanting to give her a false sense of hope.

"At this point I can't say I have anything concrete, but I do have some promising leads," he told her. "I also have a question for you."

"Yes?"

"You told me Fred's birthday was July 29, 1966 but my research came back with September 17, 1967."

Rhonda didn't respond immediately.

"Are you sure?" she asked. "There must be some mistake."

"My researcher is extremely reliable," Steve said.

"I don't know what to say, that's the date he told me and it's the date we celebrated every year. What does that mean?"

"Probably nothing. My researcher uses a computer and computers aren't perfect. I'll have him dig a little deeper."

"Please do, I can't imagine how that could happen."

"Did you ever see his birth certificate?"

"No, he said it was destroyed when his parents' house burned."

He would have needed a replacement long ago – to get a driver's license, passport, anything like that, so he must have had one. Either he didn't want her to see it or she was lying – neither option made much sense.

"Don't worry, we'll get to the bottom of it."

"What are your plans for today?" she asked.

"Since today is a normal business day, my first stop will be his office. I'll ask some questions, then I'll go wherever the answers take me."

"Please keep me updated," she requested.

"I will," Steve assured her.

The drive to the corporate offices of Halsey-Taylor took about twenty minutes. Steve parked in a visitor's parking space and entered the lobby of the three-story glass-and-steel building. A large H-T logo was displayed impressively behind the receptionist's desk and a very pleasant looking girl in her early twenties greeted him with a smile that bordered on flirtatious.

"Good morning," she said, "May I help you?"

Steve showed her his P.I. license.

"My name is Steve Salem. I'd like to talk to somebody about Fred Cranston."

"I'm sorry, Mr. Cranston isn't in yet," she said.

The news hasn't reached her yet, Steve thought.

"I don't want to talk *to* Mr. Cranston," he said politely, "I want to talk to somebody *about* him."

"Oh," she said with mild confusion, "just a moment."

She picked up the phone and dialed a three-digit extension.

"Hi, Lil," she said when her call was answered, "it's Maria. Is Mr. O'Brien available? There's a private investigator here and he wants to talk about Fred Cranston."

Maria nodded and said *uh-huh* a couple of times before hanging up.

"Mr. O'Brien, our Senior Vice-President will talk to you, his secretary is on her way."

"Thank you," Steve said.

He was looking at framed photographs of the company's more impressive projects when he heard the elevator door open. A woman who was probably fifty-five, but desperately trying to look thirty-five, stepped off the elevator and approached him with a smile.

They exchanged pleasantries and took the elevator to the third floor. At the end of a hall was a large open area dominated by u-shaped desk. On the desk was a brass nameplate reading Lillian Morgan - Executive Secretary.

On either side of the desk was a nine-foot tall, walnut door, each with a brass name plate of its own, one reading Joseph Halsey - President; the other Edward O'Brien - Senior Vice President.

"Where's Mr. Taylor's office?" Steve asked casually.

"Mr. Taylor retired six years ago," Lil said as she led him to O'Brien's door. "The company just keeps the name."

She knocked on the door and waited for a *come in* before opening it and stepping aside for Steve to enter.

A man bearing an uncanny resemblance to Tom Selleck came around an ornate, wood desk and shook Steve's hand.

"Ed O'Brien," he said by way of introduction.

"Steve Salem, nice to meet you."

"Thank you, Lil" O'Brien said as the secretary closed the door. "What can I do for you Mr. Salem? Please have a seat."

"I'm here to talk to you about Fred Cranston."

"What about him?"

"Obviously you haven't been officially notified yet, so what I'm about to tell you should remain confidential—at least for the time being."

"Of course," O'Brien agreed.

"Fred Cranston was murdered Friday night, I'm investigating on behalf of his wife."

O'Brien's facial expression showed a total lack of comprehension. The news was completely unexpected.

"Murdered?"

"Yes, he was shot."

O'Brien was speechless for several seconds.

"I'm sorry to do this after giving you such news," Steve said, "but would you mind answering a few questions for me?"

O'Brien slowly shook his head with disbelief.

"Murdered," he whispered. "Yes, of course. I'll help you in any way I can."

"Can you think of anybody, either in your company or not, who might have a reason to kill him?"

O'Brien snickered.

"That's a bit of a loaded question," he said. "Freddy wasn't the most popular guy in the company, or the industry—but only because he was good at his job, which meant not being afraid to piss people off."

"Can you be more specific?"

"To be blunt, Fred could be a real ball-buster. People tended to find him...abrasive. He called a spade a spade and he often offended people."

"Who did he offend most? Women, gays, people of certain ethnic groups?"

"He didn't discriminate. Fred usually said whatever was on his mind, regardless of his audience."

"I see, so in terms of people who may have been pushed a little too far, does anybody jump out at you?"

"Not off the top of my head. No."

Steve opened his notebook.

"Can you tell me about a man named Rick, a sub-contractor on the hospital project?"

"Just a minute," O'Brien said as he picked up the phone and called his secretary. "Lil, would you bring the sub list for the hospital?"

"I'm sorry," O'Brien said as he hung up the phone. "I don't know all of our subs. There are just too many."

"Understandable," Steve said. "Did Fred have any intense confrontations with co-workers?"

"Nothing I can think of, the occasional argument here and there—certainly nothing to warrant murder?"

"Does the name Brian Townsend mean anything to you?"

"No, nothing."

"What about CJ Miller?"

There was a distinct hitch in O'Brien's face before he answered.

"No," he said.

"Are you sure?" Steve asked. "The police will be investigating and they're bound to ask the same questions and there's a harsh penalty for lying to them."

O'Brien shifted in his chair, struggling with the question. Steve pressed.

"If they ask me what I've learned it would be in your best interest for that information to jive with theirs," he bluffed.

Contrary to television and movies, the police rarely, if ever, asked a P.I. for information, but the general public's perception of private investigators was as the saviors of the crime prevention world, coming to aid of hapless police departments everywhere. This belief was easily exploited.

Obrien sighed, "Fred was having an affair with her."

"How long have you known about it?"

"Pretty much since the beginning, more than a year now."

"Does anybody else know?"

O'Brien held his hands out, palms up.

"Who knows? Probably anybody who would listen to him. It wouldn't be unlike Fred to brag about nailing a twenty-something stripper. I suppose if there's one guy Fred would have talked to, it'd be Paul Irving, they went to college together. Paul is one of our superintendents."

"Did you ever meet her?"

"No."

Steve took out the photo of Fred and his college friends and showed it to O'Brien.

"Do you recognize any of these people?"

"Sure, that's Fred there, and this one next to him looks like Paul, it's hard to tell after all these years, but yeah, I'd say that's them."

"How about the other two?"

O'Brien picked up the picture and studied it.

"No, I'm sorry."

There was a knock on the door. Lil walked in, handed a file folder to O'Brien and left.

"What was the name again?" O'Brien asked.

"Rick, last name begins with a C, maybe Italian."

O'Brien scanned the list of sub-contractors.

"Here's one, Rick Carpionato, he owns the shell company we hired."

"Shell company?" Steve asked.

"Right. A shell company is a sub-contractor hired to provide the general contractor with a weather-tight shell—meaning four walls, windows, doors and a roof. They can do the work themselves, or sub it out, it's up to them, but they're hired to give us a building ready for interior finish."

"What's the name of his company?"

"Carpionato Shell."

"Do you have an address, phone number, things like that?"

O'Brien pulled a business card from the file.

"Here's his card, it's all there."

Steve put the card in his notebook.

"What about these men?" Steve asked, showing Ed the picture of Fred and his golf buddies.

"Sure, Brian Chamberlain and Tony Capela. They work here. The black man is a consultant engineer," he checked the list again, "Juan Bostwick."

"How can I get in touch with them?"

Ed went into a desk drawer and fished around, pulling out four business cards. He handed them to Steve.

"Call them, tell them I sent you. My card is there too."

"Thanks. One last thing," he said. "Can you tell me where I can find Paul Irving?"

"Sure, Paul is working on a conference center in Daytona Beach, near the Speedway."

Ed wrote the address down along with a phone number. Steve put the information in his notebook and stood.

"Thank you for your time, Mr. O'Brien," he said, handing one of his cards. "If you think of anything else I'd appreciate a call."

"Absolutely," O'Brien said, "and if there's anything else I can do for you, don't hesitate to call."

Once he was in his Jeep, Steve placed a call to Bill Eldredge and asked him to do a work-up on Rick Carpionato, then he drove to International Speedway Boulevard to find Paul Irving.

~TEN~

The job site of the future conference center looked more like a five-acre dirt moonscape than a construction project. There was no actual construction taking place yet and the only structure on site was a 40-foot trailer with a Halsey-Taylor sign mounted on the side. There were two men operating earth-moving equipment and two men using surveying equipment.

The entire site was surrounded by a six-foot chain-link fence. A sign at the gate directed all visitors to check in at the *construction office,* which, Steve assumed, was the trailer. As he followed a mogul-ridden path from International Speedway Boulevard to the trailer he was thankful to be in a Jeep rather than a car.

He knocked on the door and entered after being told to do so by a voice from inside.

Seated at a counter-top/desk was a tall, thin man with a full head of wavy, auburn hair. His face had a few more lines on it than it had in the photograph, but Steve recognized Paul Irving immediately.

Paul stood up and was easily eight inches taller than Steve, although he probably weighed twenty-five pounds less.

Steve introduced himself and Paul offered him a dust-covered chair.

"What can I do for you?"

"I'd like to talk to you about Fred Cranston," Steve said.

Paul's reaction was difficult to read. There was a distinct flinch of surprise, which may have been nothing more than curiosity as to why a P.I. was investigating his boss/friend. There was also a noticeable shift in his body language—from sitting in a relaxed position, hands on the arms of his chair, to tense and withdrawn with his arms folded across his chest.

Seems a bit defensive, Steve thought.

"What about him?" Paul said.

Steve decided not to reveal his hand too early.

"What can you tell me about him?"

Paul tapped his shirt pocket looking for his cigarettes, then went on an exaggerated search of the desk as he replied.

"What do you want to know?"

Steve spread his hands and smiled, no threat, "Anything you care to tell me."

Paul found his Lucky Strikes, put one in his mouth and began searching for a match.

"Fred's a good guy. We don't see much of each other, he's a suit, I got my hands in the shit. You know?"

"Right," Steve nodded, "when you do see each other, you get along?"

"Enough to say 'Hi', you know..."

He found a butane lighter under a stack of papers and lit his Lucky.

"I see," Steve said. "didn't the two of you go to college together?"

Paul flicked his ashes on the floor and rubbed them with his work boot.

"Yeah, twenty-some years ago. You know how it is, people change."

"Yeah, they sure do," Steve agreed. "Ever talk about the good old days?"

"Nope. Not a word, I guess maybe they weren't so good."

Steve nodded, hoping his silence would force Paul to keep talking.

"After graduation we hardly ever saw each other," Paul continued, "until about two years ago when I started working here."

"Did Fred get you the job?"

Paul's hand absently went to his shirt pocket again, even while it held the still-burning cigarette.

"He may have put in a word for me."

"Did you ask him to?"

"Bet your ass I did, I was up against it."

"What do you mean?"

"I called Fred after I lost my last job. My unemployment ran out, I was looking at foreclosure and I had a son ready to go to college. I knew H-T was hiring, I told him I needed a job and asked if he could help me out."

"Did he?"

"Yeah, he had no choice."

Paul ended the sentence abruptly and took a drag of his Lucky.

"You know, because we were old friends," he added.

Steve was quiet for a minute.

A minute ago he only knew him well enough to say hi, now they're old friends? And to say 'he had no choice' doesn't exactly jive. Steve thought.

"So what's this all about?" Paul asked.

Steve took out the photograph.

"Do you remember this picture?"

Paul examined the picture, nodded and handed it back.

"Sure, I remember it. I didn't think there were any pictures from that trip. It was spring break, '88. We went to Vegas. It was a good time until…"

"Until what?"

"Until Walt died."

"Which one is Walt?" Steve asked.

Paul pointed to the picture.

"That's Walt there next to me, and that's Fred with his arm around Brenda."

Steve looked at the picture again.

Something wasn't adding up.

"Fred is the one with his arm around the girl?" he asked.

"That's what I said. Of course he's put on a few ell-bees since then."

"What was Walt's last name?"

"Vest, Walter Vest."

"Who's the woman?"

"Brenda Kaiser. She was a good kid. Are you going to tell me what all the questions are about?"

"Where were you Friday night?" Steve asked.

"Friday night," Paul said. "My wife and I went to St. Augustine, stayed at a bed and breakfast."

"What was the name of it?"

"The St. George Inn," Paul said flatly. "I think it's time to tell me what's going on."

Steve stood and shook Paul's hand. He handed one of his cards to Paul.

"If you remember anything about Fred that you didn't mention I'd appreciate a call," he said.

Paul took the card and threw it on the desk.

"Yeah, sure. Of course it would help if I knew what you were looking for."

"Have a good day," Steve said as he left the trailer, closing the door behind him.

In his Jeep he made another call to Bill Eldredge, adding the names Brenda Kaiser and Walter Vest to the list and asking him to verify Paul Irving's alibi for Friday night.

~ELEVEN~

Five miles west of US Highway 1, on a deserted stretch of SR 100 in Bunnell, a small redneck bar called Rebs sat back off the road. It was the only building within five miles either way and looked as though it had been left behind by progress.

According to Ralph, it was the favorite haunt of Fred Cranston's new bookie, John Santoro.

Steve turned his Jeep into the gravel lot and parked next to a black, vintage-seventies Pontiac Trans Am. Written in gold script above the trademark hood-bird were the words *Free Bird.*

Steve glanced at the license plate, which read *Johnny S.*

"How original," he said.

From the outside, the building look abandoned. The windows were blacked out and the wood siding was badly weathered.

There were two other vehicles in the lot, a faded blue mini-van and a large pickup truck covered with mud.

Ignoring the hand-written sign on the front door—*Yankees and Niggers Keep Out*— Steve pulled the door open and stepped into the dimly lit bar. He removed his sunglasses and let his eyes adjust.

The jukebox played a country song while two men in sleeveless shirts played pool and a third man sat at the bar alone. A forty-something woman filled a cooler with Budweiser, swaying her hips to the music. A scarred and dirty Pit Bull, weighing about 125 pounds, slept in the corner.

Steve took the stool next to the man at the bar.

His dark hair was cut high and tight and for some reason, known only to him, he wore dark wrap-around sunglasses. A toothpick hung from his lips and his gut hung over his belt. There was a crude tattoo of a crucifix on the middle knuckle of his right hand. A glass of draft beer sat on the bar in front of him.

The barmaid stood in front of Steve.

"What can I getcha?" she asked.

"Draft is fine," he said.

He took a healthy swallow of beer.

"You John?" he said.

The man shifted the toothpick to the other side of his mouth.

"You talking to me?" without looking at Steve.

Great, Steve thought, *a DeNiro wannabe.*

"Nobody else here," he said.

"Fuck off."

"Fred Cranston sent me, said I could make a bet."

The man turned in his seat.

"You wanna make a bet? You see that dog over there? I'll bet he can beat you to the fucking door," he said.

"So you don't know Fred and you're not John?"

"Satan," the man said.

The Pit Bull's head snapped to attention.

Steve took another swallow of beer and dropped a five dollar bill on the bar, along with his card.

"If you see John - tell him to call me," he said before walking out.

As he drove east on SR 100, surrounded by cow pastures, cabbage patches and trees, he called Bill Eldredge and asked him to find the owner of the Trans Am. It only took him a minute to confirm the car was registered to John Santoro.

Steve hung up his phone and glanced in his rear-view mirror to see a pickup truck approaching rapidly. Expecting the truck to pass him, he moved over to the edge of the lane to give it more room. The truck moved across the center line and accelerated. In his peripheral vision Steve watched it come abreast of his Jeep, then slow to keep pace with him. He glanced over and recognized the truck as the one from the parking lot of Rebs and the two occupants as the pool players.

The man in the passenger seat flashed a tobacco-stained grin and pointed a revolver at Steve.

Instinctively, Steve slammed his foot on the brake as the man pulled the trigger. The shooter turned and yelled to the driver and the truck skidded to a stop sending thick, white smoke into the air, then began moving backward toward Steve. The rear window of the cab slid open and the passenger's face appeared, his arm sticking out pointing the revolver.

Small puffs of smoke left the barrel of the gun as it fired, but the movement of the vehicle caused his shots to go wild. Steve jammed his shifter into four-wheel-drive and drove into the ditch along the side of the road. The two vehicles passed each other going in opposite directions. Steve moved back onto the road and accelerated.

The pickup once again reversed its course and resumed chasing.

Steve's speedometer reached eighty-five and the pickup still gained. On the horizon he saw a dump truck pulling a trailer carrying a large backhoe. The gap between Steve and the slow moving dump truck closed quickly.

Time was not on his side.

The dump truck was getting closer every second and the pickup was gaining behind him just as fast.

He eased up on the gas slightly. The gap in front of him still closed, as did the one behind him. He put the gun taken from the trailer-park punk between his legs. When the pickup was less than thirty feet behind him, he swung out to the left, across the center line, and accelerated past the dump truck, the pickup followed, closing the gap to two car-lengths.

Steve's Jeep moved past the front bumper of the dump truck and the pickup was fully abreast of it. Steve pointed the gun at the left front tire and fired three rounds—then stomped his accelerator.

At least one bullet struck the tire. When it blew, it was actually louder than the gunshots had been.

The dump truck pulled violently to the left, pushing the faster-moving pickup with it. The dump skidded to a violent stop in the ditch, but the pickup's momentum wouldn't allow it to stop. It dove into the ditch and rocketed up the other bank. As it flew out of the ditch the right-front corner clipped a tree causing the ass-end to spin forward. The left rear tire hit the ground and the truck tumbled over several times before coming to a rest on its side in front of a cluster of cows, who stood motionlessly watching the action as they chewed mouthfuls of grass.

Steve kept his foot glued to the floor until he reached SR 100.

~TWELVE~

After his adrenaline levels subsided, Steve called Bill Eldredge again.

"Bill," he said, "I need whatever you can find on a second-rate bookie named John Santoro, from Bunnell."

"Everything?" Bill asked. "I'll have to charge you a little extra."

"I don't care. Use whatever resources you need, check every closet and lift every rock."

"Will do," Bill said. "Is everything okay? You sound a little flustered."

"Yeah, I had a run-in with some good-old boys, but I survived. Put Santoro on the front burner, will you?"

"Sure thing, I've got some info on the other two, Kaiser and Vest already."

"Are you busy?"

"Not especially."

"Meet me at the Lion in twenty minutes?"

"I'll be there."

Steve said hello to Ralph and Ike as he walked to the tiki bar at The Golden Lion.

Despite his general policy against drinking during the day, he ordered a shot of whiskey.

"A little early in the day for that, isn't it?"

He turned to see Bill taking the stool next to him.

"Tough morning," he said.

"Sorry to hear that."

Bill took a seat, ordered a glass of sweet tea and opened a manila folder.

"What did you find?" Steve asked.

"Before I forget, Paul Irving did stay at the St. George on Friday night. He checked in at 6:37 p.m. and checked out at 10:19 a.m. on Saturday. He ordered a bottle of wine from room service and had dinner at O.C. Whites. You want to know what they ate?"

"No, I just wanted to make sure he had an alibi," Steve said. "There's something about him that gives me a funny feeling. I don't think he's the man I'm looking for, but he's hiding something. Anyway, what have you got?"

"Brenda Kaiser," Bill said, "born 3 December, 1966 in Richmond, Virginia. Good student, no trouble with the law, made the Dean's List at Florida. Never married, had one child—a daughter—in 1989. She's pretty clean, nothing that jumps off the page—even her credit score is nearly perfect."

"Where is she these days?"

"Gainesville. She works for the City's engineering department—contact info is all in here."

"Good, thanks."

"As for Walter Vest," Bill said, "there's not much information, as you can imagine."

"I wasn't expecting much, I just want to make sure I've covered all the bases. Right now the smart money is on Santoro."

"Smart money doesn't gamble," Bill added.

"Good point," Steve said. "So what about Vest?"

"Walter Michael Vest, born 29 July, 1966…"

"Say again," Steve said.

Bill looked at his paper.

"Date of birth July 29, 1966, why?"

"Isn't that the date I had originally given you for Cranston? The one that was wrong?"

"Was it?" Bill said. "I don't recall."

"I'm not totally sure, but it sounds awfully familiar."

"Be that as it may," Bill continued, "Vest grew up in a small town outside of Pittsburgh called Sinking Spring. Attended U of F from '84 to '88, obviously never graduated. He died in April of '88, less than two months shy."

"How'd he die?"

"The official cause of death was a single gunshot wound to the back of the head."

"Execution?"

"Sounds like it, they found his body in the trunk of a rental car in the Nevada desert."

"Interesting."

"Why?"

"Two friends, both executed. What are the odds?"

"You want odds?" Bill said, "Go over there and talk to Ralph, I'm strictly information acquisition."

"That's a clever way of phrasing it," Steve said. "I don't suppose there were any arrests made in Vest's murder."

"No, but according to a newspaper article, the accepted theory was that he ran afoul of a local bookie."

"Shame," Steve said, "kid that young."

"It is, but you know what they say about playing cards with the devil."

"The devil always wins," Steve said. "I wonder..."

"Wonder what?" Bill asked.

"Two guys, college buddies, both liked to gamble, both executed. On any other day I'd say coincidence, but the date of birth thing throws a wrench in the gears. I think I'll take a ride to Gainesville and talk to Brenda Kaiser."

Bill nodded and drank some tea.

"What do you think?" Steve asked.

"I think this is good tea."

"Right," Steve said, "you're strictly information acquisition. So how soon can you have Santoro done?"

"Maybe later today, tomorrow for sure."

"Good, thanks again, Bill."

Steve finished his whiskey and left.

He programmed Brenda Kaiser's address into his GPS and headed for Gainesville.

On his way to Gainesville Steve he called Brenda Kaiser's work phone number and introduced himself as a private investigator, but gave no details as to the nature of his inquiry. She agreed to meet him at her home in two hours.

She lived in a quiet section of Gainesville, away from the congestion of the city-proper. She led him to a screened-in lanai and provided a pitcher of iced-tea. Despite the addition of about fifteen pounds, Steve recognized the attractive woman from the photograph. Unlike Fred and Paul, Brenda Kaiser had aged well.

"Thank you for agreeing to see me on such short notice," Steve said.

"Don't mention it," she said with a sincere smile. "What can I do for you?"

"Do you know a man by the name of Fred Cranston?"

Her reaction was one of surprise, but not guilt.

"Yes, I know Fred, we went to school together."

"Would you say the two of you were close?"

Her smile flickered, ever so slightly, before she answered.

"I guess so," she said. "As close as college classmates usually are."

"As best as you can remember, what kind of person was Fred?"

She blushed briefly and smiled shyly.

"Fred was a very kind person, friendly and honest. You know how they say *the guy your mother warned you about*?"

"Yeah, sure."

"Well, Fred was the guy your mother told you to search for."

Steve's surprise must have shown.

"Why do you look like that?" she asked.

"Nothing," he said, "it's just that you speak more highly of him than other people do."

"Really? I can't imagine why. Anybody who knew Fred like I did..."

She let the thought trail off.

"When was the last time you saw him?"

There was a slight delay in her response, but it wasn't because she was searching for a memory, it was more like she was remembering something fondly.

"On our Spring break trip, senior year."

"The trip to Vegas?"

"That's right, how did you know about that."

"I spoke with Paul Irving earlier."

"Oh, Paul," she said. "How is he? I miss him too."

"He seems to be doing fine, he and Fred worked for the same company."

"Good, I'm glad," she said. "It's good they stayed in touch, we were all so close."

Steve nodded.

Not quite the impression I got from Paul.

Brenda looked at him sideways.

"Did you say *worked,* past tense?"

"Yes," Steve said. "I'm sorry to tell you, but Fred was killed Friday night."

"Killed? How?"

"He was shot."

"Oh my God," she said through her hands. "He's dead? I can't…"

Despite her best efforts, she cried. Steve let her get it out of her system.

"Did you come all the way out here just to tell me?"

"No, actually I'm investigating his murder," Steve said, "for his wife."

"How did my name come up in your investigation?" she asked. "If you don't mind me asking. I'm not a suspect, am I?"

"Not at all—I'm just following the trail," he said as he opened his notebook, "I showed this picture to Paul…"

The pictures fell to the floor and Brenda leaned over to pick them up.

"I remember that night," she said, looking at the old photo. "That was fun."

She looked at the photo of Fred and Rhonda in Cabo.

"Who are these people?" she asked.

"I'm not surprised you don't recognize him," Steve said, "he did put on some weight."

"Recognize who?"

Steve looked at her waiting for a smile or a laugh to indicate she was joking.

Nothing.

"That's Fred and his wife, Rhonda in 2004."

She examined the picture, shaking her head slowly.

"I'm sorry," she said, "but that's not Fred."

~THIRTEEN~

Steve looked at Brenda Kaiser with confusion as she handed the photographs to him.

"What did you say?" he said.

"I said 'That's not Fred'," she repeated.

"You mean it doesn't look like Fred?"

"No, I mean it's not Fred—plain and simple."

Steve looked at the picture, then at her.

"How can you be so sure?"

Her face went scarlet and her eyes darted around the room.

"Brenda," Steve urged, "a friend of yours has been killed. His wife is looking for closure, if you know something, now is the time to say it."

"Excuse me," she said, leaving the room.

She returned shortly with a bottle of scotch and two glasses. She poured two fingers into one glass and offered it to Steve.

"No, thank you," he said.

She downed it in one swallow, poured another shot then sat down and looked at him like a lost child.

"It's a long story," she said.

"I've got all the time in the world," he told her.

Brenda took a deep breath and smiled uncomfortably.

"That trip to Vegas turned into something more than spring break for us, for Fred and me," she said. "The four of us—Walt, Paul, Fred and I—had always been close, but none of them ever treated me like a girl."

She laughed awkwardly.

"I don't mean that the way it sounds," she said. "I mean they didn't chase after me and try to get me into bed. We were friends and there were no expectations."

"I understand," Steve said.

"That week, in Las Vegas, Fred and I sort of hung out together while Walt and Paul went off and did their thing. Those two were all about gambling. They couldn't wait to hit the casinos, Fred and I wanted to enjoy the city, not be cooped up in a casino all week."

"So, you're saying Fred didn't like to gamble?" Steve asked.

"God, no," she said. "He said it was like throwing money away. He told Walt it was stupid because the house always wins."

So much for leopards not changing their spots, he thought.

"How did Walt take that?"

"He hated it, he insisted he knew what he was doing and he was going to go home with a sack-full of cash."

Steve had a growing uneasiness he couldn't quite identify.

"So you and Fred did your own thing?"

"Right. We had a blast together. Then, the night before Walt died, we had a few too many drinks and..."

She looked away and tears began welling in her eyes again.

"...and one thing led to another when we got back to the hotel. I'm sure you can fill in the blanks."

"I understand."

"We felt really strange about it, we swore we would never tell anybody—*ever*."

They sat in silence for several seconds.

"And that's how I know the man in that picture isn't Fred," she said.

"How is that?"

"Fred had a tattoo on the left side of his chest. I teased him about it while we were...when he took his shirt off."

"A tattoo?"

"It was the Pink Panther holding a bottle of Heineken in his right hand and a joint in his left."

Steve raised his eyebrows and smiled.

"Interesting image," he said.

"He said he had gotten it while he was in high school, on a dare."

Steve looked at the picture more closely.

"Well, there's no sign of it in this picture. Even if he'd had it removed, there'd be a scar."

"Can I see that picture again?"

"Sure," Steve said handing it to her.

She studied it for a minute then stood.

"Excuse me," she said, and went inside.

She returned several minutes later carrying a book.

"I had trouble finding it," she said, holding up a yearbook from The University of Florida.

She flipped through the pages, found what she was looking for and showed it to Steve.

It was a memoriam page dedicated to Walter Vest. In the center was his senior picture, one that had been taken several months before he died.

"Look at this picture of Walt, and compare it to the picture of the man you thought was Fred."

"It's the same man," Steve said. "So the man who was killed Friday night was actually Walter Vest..."

"...oh my God!" Brenda said.

"What?"

"I never thought about it until now, but back in the day, Fred was too young to drink."

"And?"

"Well, he and Walt sort of looked alike."

Steve looked at the picture again.

"Yeah, I suppose it's not a stretch."

"While Walt and Paul were out at the casinos, Fred borrowed Walt's ID so he could drink."

"So the man they found in the trunk of the car was Fred with Walt's ID in his pocket," Steve finished.

Neither of them spoke for several seconds.

"Why didn't Walt say anything?" Brenda asked. "Especially after all these years. Why would he keep masquerading as Fred?"

To Steve, the answer was fairly obvious.

"Gambling," he said.

"I don't understand."

"You said it yourself, Walter Vest liked to gamble, Fred didn't. If I had to guess, I'd say that Walter got in over his head and Fred paid the ultimate price for it. Then Walter took advantage of the situation and became Fred Cranston. Just like that he's out of trouble and has a clean slate."

"That would answer some questions I've always had," she said.

"Such as?"

"Fred took off the next day, rented his own car and just left—didn't say anything. Then, when we were back in school for the last few weeks he totally avoided me. I just assumed he felt uncomfortable about us sleeping together. I left messages on his machine but he never returned my calls. He didn't show up for graduation. I never heard from him again."

They sat in silence for a few minutes before Steve picked up the scotch and poured a shot into each glass.

"Jesus," he said. "I have to say, I didn't see this one coming."

"There's something else."

Steve's eyebrows went up.

"There's more?"

She nodded and looked at the floor.

"That night…it…I mean, when we…I got pregnant."

Steve sat back in his chair and downed his scotch.

"And the hits just keep on coming," he said.

"I never told Fred," she said through tears, "although, I guess in hind sight it doesn't matter…"

She cried again. Steve reached over and took her hand in his; she squeezed it to the point of pain.

~FOURTEEN~

Brenda brought herself under control and took a sip of scotch.

"I'm sorry," she said, wiping her eyes.

"No apology necessary," Steve said. "I'm sorry you had to find out this way."

"I'm actually sort of relieved," she said, "all those years, I thought he hated me."

"Do you mind if I ask what happened to the baby?"

"I put her up for adoption as soon as she was born. On her birth certificate I left the father as unknown, which was a little embarrassing at the time."

"Have you ever had any contact with her?"

"Actually, she found me a couple of years ago. She came to visit and spent a couple of days. I was amazed at how she'd grown into such a beautiful young woman."

"I'm sure that was rewarding."

Brenda nodded.

"She's so smart—she was going for her Masters in psychology with a minor in criminal justice. She said she wanted to be an FBI profiler."

"Wow, very impressive," Steve said. "Did you tell her about her father?"

Brenda shook her head.

"No, I didn't, and she never asked. To be honest, at the time I was sort of glad. I was a little uncomfortable, you know?"

"Sure," he said. "So I assume her name isn't Cranston."

"No, it isn't," Brenda said. "Her name is Casey—Valerie Casey."

The name rang a bell with Steve but he couldn't quite place it. He wrote it in his memo book.

"I think I've done enough damage here," Steve said. "Thank you for your time."

As they walked to the door he handed her his card.

"If there's anything else you can think of, please call me."

"I will," she said. "And when you figure out what happened will you let me know?"

"Absolutely," he promised.

~*FIFTEEN*~

Less than a block from Brenda's house, Steve made a call to Bill Eldredge.

"It's a good thing I'm not busy," Bill said.

"Sorry, Bill, but I've found a loose thread and I'm really curious to see what unravels when I pull it."

"What do you need from me?"

"First, I need as much as you can find on Paul Irving. Concentrate mostly on the last couple of years, since he started working for Halsey-Taylor, especially his bank records."

"Got it. Next?"

"Walter Vest—Cranston's college friend who was killed. Dig a little deeper—find out whatever you can about him from before he died, and get any details you can from the investigation into his death. I know it was an unsolved homicide, but there'll be interviews, evidence things like that. Maybe they've been computerized"

"Okay," Bill said. "Anything else?"

"Not at the moment. Have you gotten anything on Santoro?"

"Yeah, you want to meet?"

"I'm on my way back from Gainesville—my office in two hours?"

"See you there."

Bill was admiring the ocean from the shoulder of A1A, when Steve arrived.

"Been waiting long?" Steve asked.

"Ten minutes," Bill said. "You really need a partner, that way I wouldn't have to wait for you."

"I don't need a partner," Steve said, unlocking the front door.

"Okay, you need an assistant. You'd be much more efficient."

"I've got you, what more could I ask for?"

"I'm not an assistant. I told you, I'm strictly information acquisition. I can't help you assimilate the information or turn it into a working theory. Like my daughter says, 'Dad, you're smart, but you couldn't buy a clue'."

"Let's worry about one thing at a time, shall we?" Steve said as he sat behind his desk. "I'll worry about getting help later."

"Exactly my point," Bill said, flipping open a folder. "Okay, where to begin?"

He looked at the first page before handing it to Steve.

"Chris Tucker, really nothing there, the guy's pretty much clean. Although I do think he's having an affair, he uses his credit card at a lot of hotels."

"Hey," Steve said, "you assimilated."

Bill ignored the remark and continued.

"In fact, he was at a hotel in Palm Coast the night of the murder."

"I didn't really think he was our man, I was just curious because he tensed up when I asked him where he was."

"Next on the list, I found no connection between Brian Townsend and Dean Ericson, but according to the six degrees of separation theory, there's probably something, somewhere."

"Ericson is Rhonda's pool guy—Rhonda's husband was sleeping with CJ Miller and CJ Miller has some type of relationship with Brian Townsend. How many degrees is that? Four or five? Regardless, I'd bet dollars to donuts Townsend's a loner."

Bill looked at his next page.

"Richard N. Carpionato, he's been named in some criminal investigations, mostly racketeering but I'll skip the particulars, he's been in Mexico for the last nine days."

Steve took the page and put it with the rest.

"If he's mobbed-up…" Steve started

"Allegedly mobbed-up," Bill corrected.

"Yeah, right. Point is, he could have ordered the hit and the trip to Mexico is just an alibi."

Bill nodded, "I suppose it's possible."

"Anything's possible, Bill. People are capable of doing all sorts of things—good and bad—when they have the proper motivation. The scary thing is when they do something bad, they usually find a way to rationalize it."

"I understand rationalization," Bill said, "I rationalize going through a stop sign if I'm in a hurry—but murder?"

Steve spread his hands, "We all have our own definition of justice."

Bill shook his head and picked up three pages, held together with a paper clip, and raised his eyebrows at Steve.

"John Santoro," he said, "real piece of work. The fact that this guy is walking around makes me question justice."

"You should meet him in person," Steve said.

"I'll pass," Bill said as he looked at the first page. "Santoro is thirty-five years old, grew up in Denver and flew under the radar until he got out of high school, not a blip."

"And then?"

"Two months after he graduated, he beat an elderly woman into a coma and robbed her of $68."

"Lovely."

"He served twenty-eight months for that. After he was released he was promptly arrested for putting a guy in the hospital after a traffic accident. Hit him in the ribs with a baseball bat. He served another eighteen months for that one," Bill said.

"Perfect example of what I was talking about," Steve said. "I'm sure in his mind, he needed the $68 more than the woman and as far as the traffic accident…he most likely felt the other guy did something to warrant the broken ribs."

"There's a word for people like that…sociopath. Especially when you consider the accident was his fault."

"No argument here."

"Anyway," Bill continued, "he came to Florida three years ago and although he's managed to avoid prison, he's been arrested seven times for crimes ranging from armed robbery to assault with a dangerous weapon."

"No convictions?"

"No. Twice the charges were dropped by the complainant, three times there was insufficient evidence, one case was dismissed because of an illegal search and the other was dismissed because the only witness refused to testify."

"Any paper trail to alibi him out for Friday night?"

"Nothing. In fact, he doesn't leave a paper trail at all. He's got no utilities in his name, he doesn't own any property other than his car, no contracts filed, not even a cell phone. Even his driver's license is expired."

"His car is registered, there must be an address on the registration."

"I checked the county appraiser's web site, the address on his registration is a junk yard on US1 in Bunnell."

"Insurance?"

"None in his name."

"Well, he tried to send me a message after I talked to him this morning, so I must have hit a nerve. I guess I'm going to have to do some old-fashioned detective work on this one."

"I'll bet you wish you had a partner now," Bill said, as he stood to leave.

~SIXTEEN~

Steve opened a bottle of Yukon Jack and poured a double-shot over ice.

"With all due respect to Nietzsche," he said to his empty house, "after a day of chaos, order comes out of a bottle of good whiskey."

He sat in his recliner, in the dark, while the soothing jazz of John Coltrane helped with the decompression process.

The residual stress from the day's events gradually evaporated and he sifted through his thoughts, trying to put them in order.

First on the list of things bothering him; how to break the news to Rhonda about the real identity of the man she had been married to—and that was the easy part. Should he then burden her with the knowledge that this man was, at the very least, indirectly responsible for the death of an innocent man twenty-three years ago?

Past that, there was the immediate issue of finding the person responsible for killing the man known as Fred Cranston.

John Santoro seemed to be the front-running candidate, especially given the attempt on Steve's life five minutes after speaking to him.

Brian Townsend could be behind it, assuming he meant what he said in his Facebook post. This theory would mean that CJ Miller had been the actual target and Fred was most likely collateral damage.

There was also the possibility that the murder was somehow related to the death of the real Fred Cranston in Las Vegas.

Following that train of thought, Paul Irving, who was surely hiding something, would be at the top of the suspect list.

Cranston's gambling habit and Santoro's volatile nature should make it a slam-dunk, he thought.

Then, almost as if the two halves of his brain couldn't agree...*If it's such a slam-dunk, why are you concerned with Paul Irving and Walter Vest?*

Two trains of thought, heading in the same direction but on different tracks.

I'm not concerned with them – I just think it's an unusual coincidence. Contrary to what some people think, coincidences do exist.

You know better...

The CD ended and quiet filled the room.

An ice-cube shifted in his tumbler, the small sound was like thunder in the silence.

The longer he sat, the louder the silence became.

It wasn't silent at all.

He closed his eyes and heard the humming of the refrigerator, the sound of cars driving by on A1A, the rush of air through the ducts overhead, the call of several crows outside and, almost as punctuation on it all, a dog barked once in the distance.

The ice shifted again. He raised the glass, finished the liquid warmth, and then set it down on the end-table.

Mental fatigue, along with the whiskey, took its toll and his mind began to power down. Slowly, he surrendered to it.

As he drifted into sleep the two trains began to merge onto one set of tracks.

The murder of Fred Cranston seemed, at first glance, to be as simple as silence…but silence was not simple…and it was never truly silent. Sometimes it was actually quite noisy.

Every detail of this case was like another bit of noise contributing to the silence.

Listen to the details, he thought as he fell asleep.

The ringing of his cell phone seemed distant at first, like a disconnected piece of somebody else's dream. It shifted, becoming part of his own dream, but somehow he knew he wasn't dreaming and he told himself to wake up and answer the phone.

When he finally came out of the deep sleep, the ringtone was much closer, sounding more urgent than it had while he slept.

"Hello," he said without checking the caller ID.

"Did I wake you?"

"Who's this?"

"It's Bill. Boy you must have really been out."

"I guess so, what time is it?"

"Eight-thirty."

"Wow, guess I was pretty tired, I fell asleep in the recliner and didn't move all night. What's up?"

"Well," Bill said, "while you were out, pun intended, I was following up on Paul Irving and Walter Vest as per your request."

Steve shuffled to the kitchen and started a pot of coffee.

"When can we meet?"

"I have a meeting at nine," Bill said. "It'll end before ten, meet you at The Golden Lion around ten-thirty."

"I'll be there."

Steve arrived before Bill and passed the time talking to Ralph and Ike about his encounter with Santoro.

"Something needs to be done about that jerk," Ralph said. "The world would be a better place without him."

"I'm all for making the world a better place," Ike said, drawing a look of surprise from Steve, who had rarely heard him talk, "I'll take care of him."

"No, Ikey," Ralph said. "He isn't worth the risk. Don't worry—he'll get what's coming to him."

"I know he will," Ike said. "I just wouldn't mind being the delivery-man."

"With any luck," Steve said, "he'll be going to prison for murder soon."

"You think he's good for the Cranston hit?" Ralph asked.

"After yesterday," Steve said, nodding, "yeah. All I did was mention Cranston's name, and he decided I was a big enough nuisance to have killed."

Steve's cell phone rang, it was Bill Eldredge calling to say his meeting had run over and he'd be a little late. Steve told him to take his time and hung up.

"By the way," he said to Ralph and Ike, "I learned something very interesting about Fred Cranston yesterday."

"Please, share it with us," Ralph said.

Steve told them the story of Fred Cranston, Walter Vest and the apparent identity switch.

"So, this guy, Vest, loans his ID to the real Fred Cranston and when Cranston ends up dead, Vest becomes the new Fred Cranston?" Ralph asked.

"That's what I'm thinking," Steve said.

"It's not the craziest thing I've ever heard," Ralph said.

"For Vest, it was probably a no-brainer," Steve said. "We know he had gambling issues, so it isn't hard to imagine him getting himself into hot water with a Vegas bookie. The real Cranston was, by all accounts, a clean kid. When he turns up dead with an ID that says Walter Vest, the real Vest sees it as a golden opportunity. It was a simple solution for him. Cranston had no family—no past that would ever catch up to Vest."

"Identity theft at it's finest," Ike said.

"It wasn't Cranston's past that caught up to him," Ralph said, "it was his own. Gambling was in his blood and it didn't matter what he called himself, he couldn't change that."

Steve looked over Ralph's shoulder to see Bill Eldredge enter the courtyard.

"Well," he said, standing, "it's been nice talking, gentlemen, but it's back to business."

"Always a pleasure," Ralph said.

Ike nodded.

On the rooftop deck, Steve and Bill discussed Bill's findings over coffee.

"What sort of dirt did you dig up for me?" Steve asked.

"Let's see," Bill opened a folder. "I dug into the murder of Walter Vest and, because it's still unsolved, they've put all the records into the computer."

"Was there anything good?"

"As I said, Vest's murder was unsolved and it has long been assumed that it was the work of a bookie named Jack *Sonny* Fiske, mostly because they found a playing card at the scene—the Jack of Diamonds—which was Fiske's signature. Other than that there was no evidence tying Fiske, or anybody else for that matter, to the crime scene. Of course, crime scene investigation in 1988 was primitive by today's standards."

"Is that it?"

"Sorry to say, yeah," Bill said.

"Okay, what about Irving?"

"I focused on the last couple of years, like you asked. He began working for Halsey-Taylor in October of 2009, just in time to save his home from going into foreclosure. Prior to that he had been a superintendent for a construction company called Hall and White, they filed bankruptcy in June 2008. Irving collected unemployment for the next twelve months until his benefits ran out. Then, in July '09, his bank account gets a deposit of ten-thousand dollars."

"Really?" Steve said. "Did you..."

"Cross check it against Cranston's?" Bill finished. "Yes and yes, there was a matching withdrawal from his account the day before."

"And three months later Irving is working at H-T."

"Right, and I took it upon myself to look into his salary—Irving is paid about thirty-percent more than the rest of their superintendents."

"It would appear that Irving called in a couple of favors from his old college buddy."

"Is that a euphemism for blackmail?"

"More than likely," Steve said.

But why would Irving kill Cranston? Steve thought. *Santoro, at least had motive. Cranston's influence with Halsey-Taylor probably kept Irving employed, why throw that away?*

Once again, the trains diverged onto separate tracks.

On their way downstairs Steve noticed someone standing at Ralph's table, it was Ralph's nephew, the one he had seen in the bar the night of the murder.

As soon as he saw the kid the tracks converged and the individual cars joined to make one long, perfectly sensible, train. He stopped short and Bill walked into him from behind.

"What are you doing?" Bill asked.

"Sorry," Steve said. "Bill, listen, are you busy at the moment?"

"Not especially. Why?"

"Hold on for a minute," he said, taking his cell phone out.

After making a short phone call to Brenda Kaiser, he handed Bill a bar napkin.

"I need everything you can get me, as soon as possible."

Bill looked at the napkin, "Who the heck is Valerie Casey?"

"If I'm right, she's my murderer."

~SEVENTEEN~

Forty-five minutes later Bill arrived at Steve's office with his findings.

"I know I'm just the information gatherer," Bill said, "but I have to say, if this girl is a murderer..."

"Let me stop you right there," Steve said. "There's very little doubt in my mind she killed Fred Cranston and CJ Miller. She had the opportunity, the means and most of all, the motive—the trifecta."

"She had opportunity?" Bill asked.

"I didn't know it at the time, but I saw her in the bar the night of the murder."

"Means?" Bill said.

"All she needed was a gun, you can buy a gun in a pawn shop in some states without even showing an ID."

"What was her motive?"

"That would have been the missing link had it not been for my meeting with Brenda Kaiser."

Bill shook his head, "I'm not following..."

Steve began by telling Bill about the incident in the bar with Ralph's nephew and the attempted theft of Valerie Casey's purse. From there he skipped ahead to his meeting with Brenda Kaiser, the story of the death of the real Fred Cranston and Brenda's unexpected pregnancy.

"She told me her daughter's name, and I knew it sounded familiar, but I couldn't put my finger on it, until I saw Ralph's nephew earlier."

"Wow," Bill said, "just goes to show, you never can tell—especially from looking at this." He held up a few sheets of paper.

"I know most of it already," Steve said. "Adopted, excellent student, psychology major and all around model citizen."

"That's about the size of it—but if you know so much about her, and you're sure she's the one, why the workup?"

"I was hoping you'd get a hit on recent credit card usage."

"I did. Would you like to hear it?"

"Let me guess," Steve said, "she flew in to Florida last week sometime…"

"Right, last Tuesday, she flew out of Oklahoma City, stopped over in Atlanta then to Jacksonville."

"…stayed at a hotel in this area…"

Bill consulted the printouts.

"Actually, it was a bed and breakfast in St. Augustine."

"…rented a car, either a Ford Taurus or a Mercury Sable…"

"Right again, she rented a dark blue 2009 Ford Taurus at the airport in Jacksonville."

"…and she flew back to Oklahoma on Saturday or Sunday." Steve said.

Bill scanned the sheets again.

"Sorry, you should have quit while you were ahead. She hasn't left yet."

"You mean she's still here?"

"I believe so, she hasn't checked out of the bed and breakfast and she purchased dinner at Harry's last night."

She's been in town for a week, she killed two people and hasn't run yet. Why not?

Steve walked to the window and looked at the ocean. A lone pelican glided into his view, did a tight circle and dove headlong into the water. A few seconds later the bird surfaced and flew away, eating his catch as he flew. A minute later he circled around and dove in again, coming up with another fish.

The bird flew away, his hunting expedition was over.

"That's it," Steve said.

"What?" Bill asked. "What's it?"

"The reason she hasn't run yet. She isn't done."

"Steve, what are you talking about?"

"Valerie Casey didn't leave town because she still has one more target."

Sitting in his Jeep at a light on International Speedway Boulevard, Steve had a good view of the construction trailer.

Paul Irving's green and yellow company pickup truck was parked in front of it—fortunately there was no sign of Valerie Casey's Taurus.

It was looking like he would get there in time to get Irving out of harm's way.

As he waited for the light to change he wondered how Paul would feel about being the bait in a trap to catch Valerie Casey.

Half-a-mile ahead he spotted a car turning into the entrance of the site—a dark blue Taurus.

He slammed the heel of his hand into the steering wheel, trying to convince the light to change.

When it did, Steve shot away like he'd been fired from a cannon.

The Taurus moved slowly along the rutted, dirt road on the site. Steve still had a quarter-mile to the entrance. Given the position of his car compared to hers he would never get to the trailer before she did. Even if he prevented her from escaping afterward, a man would still be dead.

When he was two-hundred yards from the entrance, the Taurus was fifty yards from the trailer. He noticed a spot in the six-foot high chain-link fence that was partially collapsed, as though a car had gone off the road and hit it by accident.

Without hesitating, he jerked the wheel of the Jeep, shot over the curb and crashed through the fence. He jammed the transmission into four-wheel-drive and floored the gas.

The Jeep bounced across the barren construction site as Valerie Casey got out of her car.

His speedometer hit sixty and his teeth rattled as she climbed the steps.

He skidded to a stop in front of the trailer, killed his engine and leapt from the vehicle, drawing his gun.

Tearing the trailer door open he barged in, gun drawn, to see Valerie Casey standing in the middle of the room holding a pistol.

She was alone.

"Don't move," he ordered.

She raised her hands slowly. Steve couldn't tell if the look on her face was more disappointment or resignation. What it wasn't—was defeat.

Steve held out his left hand.

"Hand me the gun," he said.

Valerie handed him a Colt .45, he tucked it in his waistband.

"Who are you?" she asked.

"My name is Steve Salem, Miss Casey, I'm a private investigator."

She looked at him with surprise.

"How do you know my name?"

The door opened and Paul Irving entered talking into his cell phone.

"…as soon as you're done excavating for the slab..." he said into the phone. "What the fuck is going on here," he asked when he saw Steve pointing a gun at the woman.

Steve lowered his weapon and looked at Paul.

"Paul, do you remember me? Steve Salem, I was here the other day."

Irving nodded slowly, looking back and forth from Steve to Valerie.

"We need to talk," Steve said.

It took a second for Paul to respond.

"I'll call you back," he said into the phone. "Now somebody tell me what the hell is going on. What are you doing here, with a gun, and who is she?"

~EIGHTEEN~

"Is anybody going to answer me?" Paul said. "And is the gun necessary?"

Steve looked at Valerie—she shrugged as if to say he wouldn't need the gun—so he holstered his weapon.

"Good," Paul said, as he lit a Lucky Strike. "Now, are you gonna tell me what's going on?"

"You remember I was here asking you about Fred Cranston's murder?" Steve said.

"Yeah," Paul said. "What about it?"

"Well I solved it."

Paul was silent. He furrowed his brow at Steve, then looked at the woman. Valerie returned his look silently.

"Her?" Paul asked.

"That's right," Steve said, "and she was here to kill you next."

Paul's mouth opened and closed like a fish on the floor.

"Me? Why me? I don't even know her."

"Long story short, she's avenging her father's death."

"Her father? Who's her father? I've never killed anyone, why is she after me?"

"Her father was Fred Cranston."

"Fred? How...but you just said *she* killed Fred Cranston."

"No. She killed Walter Vest, but then again, you already knew that."

Irving's knees buckled slightly and his Lucky Strike fell to the floor. He placed his hand on the desktop for balance then collapsed into the chair.

Valerie looked at Steve, impressed with his knowledge.

"You know?" she said.

"Probably not all the details," Steve said, "but enough."

Steve looked at Paul.

"Twenty three years ago, in Las Vegas, you helped Walter Vest switch identities with the murdered Fred Cranston."

"And Fred was her…" Paul said, then he looked at Valerie, "…your father?"

"That's right."

"I…we didn't know."

"It's usually what you don't know that comes back to haunt you," she said.

Paul placed his elbows on the desk and rested his face in his hands. The room took on a strange quiet.

He began sniffling, fighting tears and Valerie inhaled sharply as if preparing for a fight.

"You should bury your face," she said to Paul. "Ignorance is a convenient excuse, but it doesn't alter the reality of what you did or nullify the repercussions."

Paul shook his head *no* as his tears began to morph into sobs.

"Because of what you and your friend did, Brenda had to give me up at birth. I spent the first six years of my life in foster care, never knowing who my parents were, thinking nobody loved me, wanting to die."

She took a deep breath and spoke with control that Steve had to admire.

"A six-year-old should never want to die."

Paul lifted his head.

"Did you say Brenda?"

"That's right, Brenda Kaiser."

She was not finished tearing him down and, as Steve listened, he wondered if he would be able to exercise such calm control in the same situation.

"You didn't know she was pregnant, did you? If she hadn't gotten pregnant the night before you killed my father, none of this would be happening right now."

"Hold on a second," Steve interrupted, "did you say he killed your father?"

"I don't think he actually pulled the trigger, it was probably Vest, but this one helped and they both covered it up."

"Holy shit," Steve said. "Can you prove this?"

"Ask him," Valerie said.

"Paul?"

Irving was sobbing like a little girl at this point, but he nodded his head.

"God, I'm so sorry," he said, and repeated it three times without ever looking up.

Steve looked at Valerie.

"I knew they covered it up, I didn't figure them for the actual killing. I assumed it was a Vegas bookie."

"That's what they wanted it to look like. Vest was into a bookie named Fiske for thirteen-thousand dollars and he knew they'd never let him leave town without paying. So he and his friend here executed my father, left Fiske's calling card and set it up to look like a mob hit. Then they provided tidy alibies for each other, identified the body and went on with their merry, little, pathetic lives."

"How did you figure that out?"

"I've spent the last five years investigating it."

"I spoke with Brenda, she said when you visited her, you never asked about your father."

"By the time I visited her, I knew more than she did. I didn't want to burden her with the ugly truth. She's suffered enough already."

Steve's respect for Valerie Casey was growing quickly. Unfortunately, she had killed two people and would have killed a third if Steve hadn't intervened.

"Miss Casey," he said.

"You can call me Val," she told him.

"Val, I'm very sympathetic to your situation, but unfortunately we have a problem."

"What would that be?" she asked.

"Well, for starters, you killed two people."

"And...?"

"...and, I think as a student of criminal justice you wouldn't have to ask that question."

Val laughed.

"Criminal justice?" she said. "There's no such thing. Where was criminal justice when my father was executed by people he thought were his friends? Or when my twenty-one year-old mother had to give up her first-born child?"

She pointed at Paul.

"While I was growing up with next to nothing, this asshole was probably taking his family to Disney. Where's the justice in that?"

Steve flashed-back to the frigid night in Boston when he came face-to-face with a living monster.

The terror in the eleven-year-old victim's eyes was beyond imagination.

The smirk on the face of the perp was so evil in its smug satisfaction that Steve still saw it in his sleep.

The actual act of beating the man is something he couldn't remember, the only thing he recalled was snapping out of the fury after his partner pulled him away – that and the fact that the suspect was hospitalized for three months with a dozen broken bones and a list of internal injuries a foot long.

Upon his release from the hospital, the only thing that stopped his attorneys from suing Steve and the City of Boston was an unconditional release and the dropping of all charges.

A year later the same guy raped and killed a six-year-old boy. The entire act was witnessed by the victim's eight-year-old sister, who watched from a closet.

Although he went to prison for it, one child was dead, another scarred for life and a family was destroyed by the emotional stress.

Where was the justice indeed?

As his mind returned from the memory he sensed movement from his right. Before he could process the information, Paul had lunged toward him and driven him backward into Valerie, sending them to the floor.

When Steve looked up, Paul was running from the trailer.

"Paul, don't..." Steve said as the door slammed.

They untangled themselves and jumped to the door, opening it in time to see Paul's pickup spitting dust high into the air as it fish-tailed away.

"Should we..." Val began.

"In the Jeep," Steve said.

By the time they got the Jeep moving, Paul was halfway to International Speedway Boulevard.

The Jeep bounced its way to fifty miles per hour. Valerie gripped the roll-bar with one hand and the dashboard with the other.

"Where does he think he's going?" she yelled over the wind rushing through the open cab.

"Anyplace where he's not looking at getting killed or being arrested," Steve said.

"Idiot."

Steve managed to close the gap between them to about fifty yards when the truck reached the gate.

Glancing to his left, Steve noticed a tractor-trailer barreling along International Speedway.

"Oh, shit," he said.

If Irving saw the semi, he must have thought he could make it onto the road in front of it.

He thought wrong.

Despite the driver's best efforts the massive truck plowed into the side of Paul's pickup, and then continued up and over it, crushing it like a toy and dragging it for several feet before coming to a rest.

An SUV rear-ended the tractor-trailer and three more cars slammed into each other behind that.

Steam rose from the wreckage. The only movement was from the driver of the rig, who slowly climbed down to survey the scene.

Cars skidded to a stop all around, either to gawk, or to avoid gawkers. Several small fender-benders resulted.

Steve stopped the Jeep twenty yards short of the gate.

"Holy shit," he said.

"I guess there is some justice after all," Valerie said.

~NINETEEN~

Thirty minutes later Steve and Val leaned against the hood of the Jeep while a platoon of State and local police swarmed over the accident scene like ants.

Neither had spoken since the accident.

Valerie barely took her eyes from the remains of Paul's truck until they loaded his body into the coroner's wagon.

Steve watched her watching the scene. There was a strange calmness about her amid the surrounding chaos.

Two State Troopers stood at the gate in conversation, one of them pointed in Steve and Val's direction.

"Looks like they'll be coming to talk to us," Steve said.

"So it does," she replied.

"You know I'll have to tell them the truth."

"Do what you have to do."

A trooper the size of a bus approached them with a pad and pen at the ready.

"Hi folks," he said, "I'm trooper McCarroll. Did you witness the accident?"

"Yes we did," Steve answered, Valerie nodded.

"Can you tell me what you saw?"

"He drove into the road without even slowing down. The trucker had no chance to avoid him."

The trooper looked at Val.

"Ma'am?"

"That's true."

"We have a report that says you were chasing him. Is that true?"

"Chasing isn't exactly the best word," Steve said, looking at Val and shrugging, "I'd say following."

"Why were you following him?"

Steve showed the trooper his ID.

"I'm investigating a homicide and I wanted to interview him."

The trooper scrutinized the ID, looked at Steve with the "cop stare" designed to get people to talk. It didn't work.

"Is she with you?" he asked.

"Yes she is."

The trooper handed them each a blank report sheet and a pen.

"Would you please fill these out, write down what you saw? Bring them to me when you're done."

"Yes sir," Steve said.

The trooper touched his finger to the brim of his campaign hat and walked away.

"What happened to telling him the truth?" Val asked as they wrote their statements.

"I didn't lie," Steve said. "It isn't my fault he asked the wrong questions."

"You said you wanted to interview him—that was a lie."

Steve stopped writing and looked at her.

"Well, I'll be a son-of-a-bitch," he said, "I think you're right. Should I call him back and tell him?"

She smiled.

"No, he's got enough to worry about at the moment."

"Right," he said as he resumed writing.

Trooper McCarroll gave his card to each of them when they returned their statements, asking that they call him if they remembered any new or additional information.

"So," Valerie said, "what now?"

Steve handed her the gun he had taken from her.

"The way I see it," he said, "without the murder weapon, I cannot prove conclusively that you killed the man known as Fred Cranston. His wife will collect his life insurance policy and inherit his pension and all of his real property so justice has been served. My investigation is closed."

"What about Irving?"

Steve turned and looked back at the wreckage.

"A horrible accident."

Valerie looked at him with appreciation.

"You're a good man," she said.

"So I've been told."

"Give me a ride to my car?" she asked.

"I'll do better than that," Steve said. "There's a good Mexican restaurant right up the road, I haven't had lunch yet and I'm starving. Interested?"

She stopped and grinned at him.

"Mr. Salem, I'm young enough to be your daughter," she said.

"It's only lunch," he said with a wink, "and let's agree on younger sister."

She followed him to the restaurant and they ate on the patio listening to a live Mariachi band.

The primary topic of discussion was Steve's investigation. He told her about seeing her in the bar, the stolen purse incident and the credit card with her name on it.

"When Brenda told me your name, I knew I'd heard it somewhere before, but it took me seeing Ralph's nephew to jog the memory," he explained.

"Who's Ralph?"

"Ralph Donabedian, he's a local bookie. He owns my favorite restaurant. We have an unspoken agreement, I don't ask him if he breaks the law and he doesn't tell me."

"A new twist on *don't ask – don't tell* but it works. So I'm not the first criminal you've turned a blind eye to?"

"First one today."

She opened her mouth to respond but was interrupted by the ringing of Steve's cell phone. He unclipped it from his belt and looked at the display.

"What do you know?" he said. "Rhonda Cranston."

He answered the call.

"Hello Rhonda,"

"Steve, I'm sorry to bother you," she said, with more than a little fear in her voice. "but you told me to call you anytime I saw something unusual."

"It's okay, Rhonda. What's wrong?"

"I think somebody is following me."

The announcement took him by surprise, since the case was essentially over.

"Why do you say that?"

"This morning, I went to the market and I noticed a car in the parking lot. I didn't pay it much mind, but I saw it again at the gym and then again when I had my nails done."

"Are you sure it's the same car?"

"Positive, there's no mistaking it."

"Why is that?"

"Because it looks like the car Burt Reynolds drove in that old movie—Smoky and the Bandit."

Santoro's Trans Am, Steve thought. *Not a good thing.*

"Rhonda, where are you now?"

"I'm in the smoothie shop on State Road 100."

"Are there other people there?"

"A few, and the kids working."

"Is the car there?"

"I don't know, I'm calling from the ladies' room."

"Listen to me, Rhonda, I'll be there in less than thirty minutes. Stay there. Do you understand?"

"Yes, yes," she said. "I won't leave."

Steve replaced the phone on his belt and waved to the waitress for the check.

"What's going on" Valerie asked.

"I told you about the thug who tried to have me killed?" he said as he threw thirty dollars onto the table and stood up. "He's been following Rhonda Cranston all morning. She's terrified. I've got to go get her."

Val stood up.

"My car should be okay here, right?" she said.

"What?" he asked.

"I'm going with you," she said, walking away, leaving no chance for discussion.

~TWENTY~

"Listen, Miss Casey..." Steve began as they climbed into the Jeep.

"Val," she said.

"Okay, listen, Val, there's no need for you to come with me. You've accomplished what you set out to accomplish, you're free to go."

"It's not that simple," she said.

"It is that simple. Nobody knows about you, I won't say anything and the only person who could link you to the victim just died. The odds of the police finding you are remote, at best."

"That isn't the point."

"Then what is the point?"

"Mrs. Cranston is being stalked by this Santoro guy, right?"

"Possibly, it could be coincidence."

"Coincidence is nothing more than a nudge from the Gods of destiny," she said.

"Who said that?"

"I did, weren't you listening?" she said with a grin.

He returned the smile.

"Regardless of whatever is happening with Santoro and Rhonda, it still doesn't involve you."

"I disagree," she said. "If you hadn't been poking around into this case, Santoro would have no interest in Rhonda Cranston. If anything happens to her, it's partially my fault—so if I can help prevent it, I will."

"If you're sure..."

"I'm sure."

The smoothie shop was at the east end of a large strip mall. Steve parked at the west end to avoid being seen. They walked slowly toward the shop, using parked cars to shield their approach, in case Santoro was lurking.

"Santoro drives a black Trans Am, gold hood bird," he told Val.

"How discrete," she said.

"Yeah, this guy's about as discrete as a fire truck," Steve said.

They worked their way around a McDonald's next to the smoothie shop and scanned the parking lot.

"No sign of the Trans Am," Val said.

"There's Rhonda's car next to the two Harley's."

They walked quickly to the door of the smoothie shop and went inside.

A high school girl was washing tables, humming happily to the piped-in tropical soundtrack.

"Hi there," she said with a big smile. "How are you today?"

"Fine, thanks," Steve said as they moved past her toward the counter.

Aside from the girl washing tables, there was one kid behind the counter. That was it, no customers.

"Val, would you…" Steve began.

"…check the ladies' room?" she finished. "I'm on it."

"Excuse me," Steve said to the kid behind the counter.

"What can I get for you?" he said.

Val returned from the ladies' room shaking her head.

"Empty," she said.

"Shit," Steve said, then to the kid behind the counter…"I was supposed to meet a woman. Early forties, long brown hair, pretty…she called me half-an-hour ago from here. Have you seen her?"

"Yeah sure," the kid said, "she sat in that booth under the TV. She left about ten, fifteen minutes ago."

"Alone?"

"No, some dude came in and got her."

"Tall, black guy with tattoos?"

"No," the kid shook his head, "this guy was white, short, kinda dumpy, wearing wrap-arounds and chewing a toothpick, strutting like he was the shit."

"Damn it." Steve said as he tossed the kid a five.

Outside, they did a walk-around of the building and then went back to the Jeep.

"What do you know about this guy?" Val asked.

"Not enough. He's a second-rate bookie—a low-rent punk with delusions of grandeur. He lives off the grid, I can't get a location on him. I have no idea where he'd take her."

"Maybe we should start with *why* he would take her. Start with what you know...that's my philosophy."

Steve started the Jeep and headed toward his office.

"There's no obvious reason for Santoro to grab Rhonda."

"Maybe not," Val said, "but it's obvious to me that the first connection is you. You were working for her and you hassled him about her husband."

"You think he went after her to get back at me? I don't see it. He had two guys try to run me off the road ten minutes after I talked to him. If he was looking to settle a score with me, he'd come straight up the middle."

"Then there has to be another reason he'd go after Rhonda, something to do with her husband."

"It's got to be money, Santoro started taking Fred's bets after Ralph stopped. If Fred owed him a substantial amount, he might try to get it from Rhonda."

"Makes sense," Val said. "Maybe we should check her house. He might take her there hoping she's got the cash."

"Can't hurt," Steve said.

There was no sign's of life at Rhonda's house.

Steve tried the front door—locked—and Val went to the back.

"Everything's locked back there," she said.

Steve took his phone out and called Bill Eldredge.

"Okay," he said, replacing the phone on his belt, "Rhonda uses the Sun Trust Bank. Her home branch is not far from here. There's been no activity on her account today."

"If he takes her there to get the money, we might still have time," Val said.

Steve parked in the lot of a pizza parlor with a clear view of the bank's entrance. They watched the bank for an hour until they saw the manager lock the door with no sign of Rhonda Cranston.

"I think we need another plan," Val said.

"I agree. I think we need another perspective too, and I know where to get one."

"Ralph and Ike," Steve said, "this is Valerie Casey."

Val shook hands with them and Steve noticed her eyes linger for an extra beat on Ike.

"Nice to meet you," she said.

"To what do we owe the pleasure?"

"I've got a situation with John Santoro."

Ralph and Ike exchanged a look.

"I'm getting really sick of hearing that name," Ralph said. "What has he done this time?"

Steve explained the situation to Ralph.

"I keep saying it," Ralph said, "something has to be done about him."

Ike nodded and drank from a bottle of Budweiser.

"Right now, my primary concern is to get Rhonda Cranston away from him—safely—but I don't know where to look. After that, I don't care what happens to him."

"Have you tried calling Rhonda's cell phone?" Ike asked.

Steve and Val looked at each other wondering why they hadn't thought of it.

"I guess we were so busy trying to think of ways to find her, we overlooked the obvious," Steve said.

He dialed Rhonda's number, put the phone on *speaker* and placed it on the table.

"Hello," Rhonda answered after four rings.

From the background noise Steve could tell her phone was also on speaker.

'Hi Rhonda, it's Steve Salem. How are you?"

"Hello, Mr. Salem. I'm fine, um, how are you?"

"Very good, thank you. I'm calling about our appointment this morning, did you forget?"

There was a distinct hesitation before she answered.

"You know what?"" she said. "I completely forgot, I'm sorry. I hope I didn't inconvenience you."

"Not a problem. Can we reschedule? I have some news for you."

Another pause.

"That would be fine. Can I call you later? I'm very busy at the moment."

"That'll work," he said. "I'll talk to you soon."

He ended the call.

"No doubt, she's in trouble," he said to the others. "She never calls me Mr. Salem and we didn't have an appointment this morning."

"At least we know she's alive," Val said.

"It doesn't do us much good if we can't find her," Steve said. "Bill did a complete computer search on Santoro and the only address he was able to come up with was the junk yard on US1."

"Sounds like that's where we need to start looking," Val said.

"I agree," Ike said, with a wink at Val, who smiled and blushed slightly.

Ralph grinned at Steve.

"I don't know where you found her, Steve," he said, "but it's about time you got yourself a partner."

"She's not my partner," Steve said.

"Maybe she should be," Ralph said. "If you need anything, you let me know."

"Thanks, Ralph," Steve said. Then to Val he said, "Ready?"

"We're wasting time here," she said.

~TWENTY ONE~

"This is the junk yard," Steve pointed at the *Google Earth* image on his computer screen. "Once it gets dark, we'll park in the parking lot of this bar, follow these railroad tracks to the back side and work our way in to see what we can see."

Val nodded.

"In the meantime," he said, "we'll go get your car and then get your stuff at the B and B. You can crash here."

"Cool," she said.

On the way to Daytona to pick up Val's car, they drove by the junk yard. Despite the half-mile of frontage on US1, the view into the yard was completely obscured by thick trees and underbrush, with the exception of a thirty-foot chain-link gate at the entrance.

Through the fence they saw a handful of grungy trailers, a few pickup trucks and a sea of dead cars and trucks.

"Any sign of a black Trans Am?" Steve asked as he did his best to watch the road and look into the junk yard at the same time.

"I didn't see it, but I did see movement near one of those pickups, so somebody's in there."

They drove to Daytona, picked up Val's car, then to St. Augustine for her belongings at the bed and breakfast and back to Steve's house where he showed her the guest room.

After she changed her clothes they prepared to leave.

Steve took a small duffle bag from a closet.

"What's in that?" she asked.

"Surveillance gear," he said. "Let's get going, it's getting dark."

They left the Jeep in the parking lot of a biker bar and followed railroad tracks for a mile before the trees began to thin. The rising moon illuminated piles of junk cars and the smell of smoke wafted toward them. In the distance they heard the barking of dogs.

At the edge of the railroad right-of-way they came upon the six-foot high perimeter fence, it was topped with rusted strands of barbed wire.

They followed the fence until they found a spot where the ground under it was thick and sandy. Steve used his hands to dig out a trough in the sand which allowed them to crawl underneath.

Staying concealed in the piles of cars, they followed a rutted road through the yard. The barking dogs seemed to be getting closer. Without communicating, they both drew their guns, almost simultaneously.

"I love dogs," Val whispered, "but I have a feeling those dogs aren't cuddly and lovable."

Steve nodded his agreement.

They reached a fork in the road and knelt behind the rotting carcass of a school bus. Steve strained to remember the aerial image of the yard.

"If I remember correctly, left will take us out to US1, right takes us deeper into the bone yard."

"Right it is," Val said.

They moved along the right fork, leaving the scrap heaps behind and moving into thicker trees. Even though they moved further from the heart of the junk yard, the smell of smoke and the sound of dogs seemed to get closer. They also heard another sound that seemed out of place.

"Is that what I think it is?" Val asked.

"Sounds like people having a party," Steve said.

They reached a clearing where more than twenty vehicles were parked—mostly oversized pickup trucks, but also cars, SUVs and one black Trans Am.

"What the hell is going on?" Val asked. "Klan rally?"

"I wouldn't be surprised," Steve said.

Staying in the trees at the edge of the clearing they came upon the source of the noise.

Connected to the parking area by a small path was a second clearing. Dozens of people gathered around in a large open pit shouting and cheering. At each corner of the clearing a fire burned in a barrel. A generator ran, sending power to stands of halogen lights.

The sounds of barking and growling dogs competed with the noise of the crowd.

"I have a bad feeling about this," Steve said.

He motioned for her to follow and they inched to the edge of the trees. Across the clearing, behind the crowd were several cages, about three feet square, each one housing a growling or barking Pit Bull.

The crowd let out a climatic cheer and then quieted. A minute later, the crowd parted and a man walked from the center carrying the carcass of a dog. He walked to a nearby pickup and threw it in the back.

"Don't tell me," Val said.

"Dog fighting," Steve said.

He pointed at the crowd.

"There's Santoro," he said. "Looks like he's taking bets for the next fight."

"This guy is scum," Val said.

"No argument here. I don't see Rhonda."

"There were some trailers out by the road, maybe she's in one of them."

"Sounds like a good theory. Let's go see what we can find while the boys are busy."

They worked their way back to the fork in the road and followed it to the hub of the yard. There were four single-wides arranged around the perimeter of a dusty clearing. Crouched behind a tow truck they scanned the area. None of the trailers showed signs of occupancy.

"You take two and I'll take two?" Val said.

"I'm not thrilled about splitting up," Steve said.

Val took out her .45 and racked the slide. "I can handle myself."

"Okay, I'll take those two."

Steve trotted across the clearing and stood outside the door of the first trailer, listening for any sounds from the inside—there were none. He turned the knob and opened the door.

Moonlight through filthy windows barely illuminated the interior. The main room was wall-to-wall shelves, each shelf loaded with used car parts. Everything from distributor caps to hubcaps.

There was a room on each end of the trailer, the first was full of auto glass and the second with headlights, tail lights, roof-mounted lights, fog lights and every other type of light imaginable.

No sign of Rhonda Cranston.

Outside the second trailer he heard muffled sounds of human occupancy.

He crouched and walked slowly around the trailer to pinpoint the location. It sounded as if there was somebody in the room on the left end. He went back to the door and opened it slowly and quietly. The inside of the trailer was dim and dirty and the air was foul.

From the left room came the distinct sounds of two people engaged in some sort of sexual activity.

Steve crept to the partially open door and peered in.

A man lay naked on a stained mattress, head back and moaning while the head of a pear-shaped woman bobbed up and down in his lap.

"Damn, girl," the man said, "if you don't give the best head in the county."

His compliment must have inspired her to increase her efforts because he moaned even louder.

Steve pushed the door fully open and stepped into the room pointing his gun at the man.

"What the fuck?"

"What's wrong, baby?" the woman said.

She followed his eyes to Steve.

"Oh, shit," she said.

"I'm looking for a woman," Steve said.

The man's eyes went to the woman kneeling on the floor.

"No, not that woman. I'm looking for a woman who doesn't want to be here."

"Other room," the man said.

Steve picked up the man's flannel shirt and tossed it to him.

"Tear that into strips," he ordered, "then tie her hands and gag her."

Once the woman was secured he pointed his gun toward the other room.

"Let's go," he said.

The naked man led the way to the opposite end of the trailer and opened the door. They stepped into the room where Rhonda Cranston lay bound, gagged and blindfolded on a bare mattress. The presence of somebody in the room launched her into panic and she tried to push herself back away from the intruder, only to be stopped by the wall.

Steve slammed the butt of his gun into the back of the man's head—dropping him to the floor with a grunt.

"It's okay, Rhonda," Steve said calmly. "It's me, Steve."

Some of the fear went away and she began crying. Steve removed the blindfold and gag, then untied her hands.

She threw her arms around him and sobbed hysterically.

"It's okay," he said. "Come on, we have to leave."

He led her out of the trailer and across the yard where Val waited next to a tow truck.

"Rhonda Cranston," Steve said, "this is Val Casey, she's working with me."

The two women said quick hellos.

"I didn't know you had a partner," Rhonda said as they started walking.

"I don't," Steve said, "this is a temporary arrangement. I'll explain later."

Val led the way to the railroad tracks with Steve following, holding Rhonda Cranston by the hand.

The sound of the dogs and the crowd faded into the night.

"That asshole really needs to pay," Val said.

"He will," Steve said, "one way or another, he will."

~TWENTY TWO~

"Are we safe here?" Rhonda asked, looking around Steve's office nervously.

"For the time being," Steve said. "Try to relax."

Val came from the kitchen with three cups of hot tea. Rhonda clutched hers as though it were the Holy Grail.

Steve gave her a few minutes to collect herself before asking her to tell him what had happened.

She drank some tea and nodded.

"I was waiting for you in the smoothie shop, like you told me, and this man comes in and tells me that he hit my car in the parking lot, so I should come outside and wait for the deputies."

"I didn't think he was that clever," Steve said.

"Once we were outside he pointed a gun at me and told me to get in the car. He took me to that junk yard and tied me up. He said Fred owed him a lot of money and I was going to get it for him."

"Did he say how much?"

Her eyes opened wide.

"Two-hundred-thousand dollars."

"Wow," Val said, "that's a lot of bets."

"Are you sure about that?" Steve asked.

"Positive, he kept repeating it. I'm sure."

"What happened next?"

"He gagged me and threw me in that room. I was there for hours, and then you came."

"Nobody else spoke to you while you were there?"

"Nobody."

"Did you hear anything else that might be useful?"

"No, the only other thing I heard was him talking to somebody about laundry and then he left, he said it was time for the fights."

"Two-hundred-thousand dollars is far too much money for traditional gambling debts. Unless the bettor has an enormous line of credit, no bookie would let him get that far behind—especially a minor leaguer like Santoro."

"You think the money was for something else?" Val asked.

"It had to be," he said.

"Loan-sharking?" she offered.

"I thought about that, but I don't think Santoro has the clout to come out of pocket with two-hundred grand."

"Does it matter what the money was for?" Rhonda asked.

"Whatever the money was for," Steve said, "Santoro believes your husband owes it to him. Nothing will change Santoro's belief that it is rightfully his."

"Especially now," Val added, "he seems like the type to stand on pride. He's going to want the money as a matter of principle, if nothing else."

"And you won't be safe until we convince him otherwise."

"Can't we call the police?" Rhonda asked.

"And tell them what?" Steve said. "You could report him for kidnapping and false imprisonment, but I guarantee you he'd have fifteen people lining up to alibi him out."

"Then he'd be even more pissed," Val said.

"So what do I do?" Rhonda said.

"If you want me to handle it," Steve said, "I'll find a way to make Santoro go away."

"We…" Val said.

Steve looked at her with an unasked question.

"You heard me," she said.

"Okay," Steve said, "*we* can make him go away."

Rhonda finished her tea.

"Do whatever you have to do," she said.

They spent the night at Steve's house.

In the morning they drank coffee on the deck. Rhonda excused herself to go inside and when she returned she was holding Steve's phone.

"Your phone was ringing," she said as she handed it to him.

"Who ever it was left a message," he said.

He listened to the message and looked at the women.

"Listen to this," he said.

He pressed a couple of buttons and held the phone up. John Santoro's voice came from the phone.

"You think you're something, don't you asshole? Your stunt on the road the other day put two of my friends in the hospital and one of them might never walk again. Then you come to my place last night, give another one of my boys a concussion, and take something that don't belong to you. I ain't through with you and I will get what's coming to me."

The line went dead.

"He's got anger issues," Val said with a laugh.

"Yeah," Steve said, "but he's right about one thing."

"What's that?" Rhonda asked.

"He's definitely going to get what's coming to him."

~TWENTY THREE~

"I hate to do this," Steve said, "but there's something else we need to talk to you about, Rhonda."

"Yes?"

"It's about Fred and some of the things my investigation uncovered."

"Okay," she said.

"The story actually begins when Fred was in college…"

When Steve and Val finished the story Rhonda sat in silence, fighting tears and shaking her head.

"This is just…I can't believe it," she said. "Isn't it possible you've made a mistake?

"No," Val said. "I've had my DNA tested against the blood samples taken from the victim, it was a perfect match."

"And as you know," Steve said, "your husband was sterile."

"My husband," Rhonda spat. "It was bad enough when I thought he was unfaithful. Now I learn that he killed a man, and lied to me all those years. What kind of person would do such a thing?"

"I'm sorry to put this on you, especially after all you've been through in the last week," Steve said.

Val moved next to Rhonda on the sofa and put an arm around her shoulders. Rhonda leaned into her and sobbed.

"You poor thing," she said to Val after regaining some control, "you're so young and you've been through so much because of my husband."

"I'm fine," Val said. "To be honest, I'm relieved to have the truth out in the open."

"No," Rhonda said, "that's not enough. I'm going to make it up to you, or at least try."

"Rhonda, that isn't necessary."

"It is for me—my husband owes you a life—I can't make up for the past twenty-two years, but I can be there for you from now on."

They hugged again and this time Val joined Rhonda in the crying.

They went to The Golden Lion for breakfast. Rhonda regained her composure more quickly than Steve would have imagined and he was impressed with her grace under so much pressure.

"I think you should find a safe place to stay until this is cleared up," Steve said.

"Where would I go?" she asked.

"Do you have any friends or relatives you could stay with?"

"Not really, nobody close anyway."

Steve looked across the courtyard and had an idea. After they finished breakfast he led them to Ralph Donabedian's table where the bookie sat with his right-hand man, Ike.

After introductions were made Steve got to the point.

"Ralph, you said if I needed help..."

"What do you need?"

"I'd like to get Rhonda someplace where I know she'll be safe."

Ralph discretely looked at Ike, who nodded immediately.

"I know just the place," Ralph said as Ike stood.

His 6'-6", 275 pound frame dwarfed Val and Rhonda. Even Steve, at 6'-0", 210 seemed small next to Ike.

Val's eyes roamed from his feet to his face then down to the tattoo on his left forearm—a skull with a vicious-looking snake wrapped around it and poking out through an empty eye socket - the words *Death Before Dishonor* scripted on a ribbon above and below it.

"Follow me," he said as he walked toward a vintage Harley-Davidson.

"Anywhere," Val said softly.

An hour later they were at the St. Augustine Municipal Marina aboard a 37-foot boat called *The Knight's Mare*.

Ike handed Rhonda a key.

"This is the key to the door, you make yourself at home. I live here, but for the time being I want you to consider it your home, I'll crash at Steve's place."

He looked at Steve for approval.

"No problem," Steve said.

Ike packed some things in a duffel and left.

"I'll talk to you later," he said to Steve on his way out.

"Thanks, Ike," Steve said.

"Are you sure we can trust him?" Rhonda said, after Ike had left.

"Ike?" Steve said, "with your life."

"That's pretty much what I'm doing," Rhonda said.

"I'd trust him with whatever he wants," Val said with exaggerated lust.

Steve and Rhonda looked at her with surprise.

"What?" she said, "did you see those eyes?"

"I wasn't paying attention," Steve said.

~TWENTY FOUR~

After giving Rhonda specific instructions about maintaining a low profile, Steve and Val went to Steve's office, gathered a few items, then drove to a small pond on US1 with a semi-concealed view of the entrance to the junk yard.

They sat on a dock with fishing poles so as not to look out of place.

Steve trained his binoculars on the entrance and they waited.

"Okay," he said an hour later, "Santoro and another guy are talking outside the trailer. I remember the guy from the other night. He seemed to be somebody Santoro trusted, maybe his second-in-command. The other guy is getting into a pickup…"

"What a shock," Val commented.

"…and leaving. Santoro's staying behind, let's go."

They gathered up the fishing poles, which were not even strung, and threw them in the Jeep, then took off after the pickup.

They followed the truck to a liquor store. After the driver went inside Val climbed out of the Jeep.

"You know what you're doing?" Steve asked.

"Do you mean '*Can I get a tobacco chewing, beer drinking redneck to follow me to my broken down car?*'..." she said as she made adjustments to her breasts, "…Yeah, I think I can handle it."

Steve got out of the Jeep and stood a short distance away. When Val walked around the corner, followed by the guy from the junkyard, Steve turned his back to them and knelt down to tie his shoe.

"It's right here," Val said. "I don't know what happened, it was fine when I pulled in, then...nothing."

The man placed his twelve-pack of Lite beer on the ground.

"Let's have the key," he said.

"Key?" Val said.

"Well, yeah, how can I see if it'll start without the key?"

"I've got the key, right here," Steve said.

The man turned around to come face-to-face with Steve. When he looked down at Steve's hand he saw a .45 instead of keys.

"What the..." he said turning back to Val, who was pointing her pistol at him as well.

"Okay, Billy-Bob," she said, "get in your truck and drive."

Steve poked his gun into the man's ribs.

"Move," he said. "I'll keep you company."

Val drove the Jeep, following the pickup to a secluded place along a power company easement.

Using plastic zip-ties, they secured the man to the base of one of the massive poles supporting the power transmission lines. Once he was secured, Steve removed the man's work boots and socks.

"What's your name?" Steve said.

The man looked at him with macho defiance and said nothing.

"His name," Val said, "or at least what he likes to be called...is Buckshot."

"Shut the front door." Steve said.

"Have I ever lied to you, that you know of?" Val said, with a smile.

Steve smiled.

"Okay, Mr. Buckshot," he said, "this is the deal. If you tell us what we want to know, we won't kill you. Does that sound fair to you?"

"Fuck all y'all," Buckshot said.

Steve walked to a nearby mound of dirt and lightly brushed it with his foot. Instantly, thousands of ants swarmed to the top of the mound to defend against the intruder.

Steve went back to Buckshot, who continued to look at Steve with defiance.

"John Santoro seems to think Fred Cranston owes him two-hundred grand," Steve said. "Why is that?"

No response.

Steve walked to the Jeep and returned with a can of Coke. He poured some on the ground near the ant hill.

"Damn, those fire-ants will eat just about anything won't they?" he said.

Buckshot flicked his eyes to the ants then back to Steve, still not showing any concern.

"Come on, Buckshot," he said, "a punk like Santoro isn't worth it. Just tell me what I need to know and you can get to that twelve-pack."

"I got no idea what you're talking about," Buckshot said.

Steve poured some more coke, this time in a line heading for Buckshot's bare feet. He stopped six inches shy.

"No idea at all?" he said.

Buckshot watched the ants swarm toward him.

"Are you allergic to fire-ant bites, Buckshot? I've heard they can kill you."

A drop of sweat appeared on Buckshot's forehead. Steve began tipping the soda can again, this time directly over Buckshot's foot.

"Last chance, Buckshot."

"All right, all right, I'll tell you."

"Outstanding," Steve said. "Apparently you're not as stupid as you look. Now what do you know about Fred Cranston?"

"Cranston got in to Johnny deep, betting on football. Guy couldn't pick a Sunday winner on Monday. He told Johnny he didn't have the cash so Johnny tells him he's gonna have to pay it back another way."

"What way?"

"Laundering money from the dog fights."

"How?"

"By pretending to hire my company to work on his construction projects."

"What's your company?"

"We do excavation, set underground pipes, lay sprinkler systems, things like that."

"So Fred hires your company and pays you for work that you never do, using the winnings from the dog fights?"

"That's about it."

"So I take it Santoro had already given Fred two-hundred grand before he was killed."

"Yeah, and nobody knows where the money is, that's why we took his old lady, we figured she might know."

"Buckshot, we appreciate your honesty," Steve said as he walked toward the Jeep.

"Hold on a second," Val said.

Steve stopped and tuned around. Val walked to Buckshot, lifted his shirt and removed a revolver from his belt and then took his cell phone. She handed the items to Steve and took the soda can from him.

"You assholes think letting dogs fight to the death is fun?" she said looking into Buckshot's eyes. "Tell me how much fun this is."

She poured the rest of the soda onto Buckshot's bare feet, freshened the trail to the anthill, then she kicked the top of the mound again to increase the fury of the guard ants.

As she walked to the Jeep she dropped the soda can on the ground in front of Buckshot and looked into his eyes.

"It's a dog-eat-dog world, asshole."

~TWENTY FIVE~

"You've got a mean streak," Steve said as they drove away.

"No," she said. "Mean is killing defenseless animals for sport. What I did is justice."

"We did tell him we wouldn't kill him."

"If he holds his feet off the ground until he figures a way out of the zip ties he'll be fine. I can't be responsible if he's too stupid to figure that out."

"Remind me never to piss you off."

"Don't ever piss me off," she said. "Now what are we going to do?"

"I think our first priority should be to figure out where Fred hid the money."

"Makes sense, I'm thinking we start with his mistress's house."

"I agree."

"You're just saying that so you won't piss me off."

CJ Miller's house was a small two bedroom just across the railroad tracks Steve and Val had followed to get to the junk yard.

On an initial drive-by they noticed no signs of life. The grass—or weeds in this case—was a foot high, there were four newspapers in the driveway and the mailbox was open, but empty.

"Looks like somebody's been checking her mail," Val said.

"Or stealing it," Steve added.

He turned the Jeep around and went back to the house.

"I'll check the front door," Steve said, "take a look around back."

Val was out of the Jeep and moving before he finished speaking.

To no surprise, the front door was locked. He lifted the mat, lifted the dirt-filled pots where plants had once lived and felt along the top of the door trim. No hidden key.

As he was about to begin searching for a fake-rock key hider the front door opened. He jumped slightly and reached for his gun.

"Nervous?" Val said. "Looks like somebody beat us to it. Sliding glass door was shattered."

"Let's take a look around."

The furniture, or what was left of it, was destroyed. Torn sofa cushions were strewn about the living room and the entertainment center was turned over. The contents of every drawer and cabinet in the kitchen littered the floor and the bedrooms were torn apart from top to bottom.

They stood in the master bedroom examining the carnage.

"If the money was here, they would have found it," Val said.

"It looks that way."

Val went to the closet where CJ Miller's entire wardrobe had been dumped onto the floor. Using her foot, she moved aside leather mini skirts, sequin-covered tops and several shoes—all with three inch stiletto heels.

"Not exactly business attire," she said.

"It is for her business," Steve said as he looked inside the closet.

As he backed out he glanced up.

"Hold the phone," he said, walking out of the room quickly.

He came back with a small make-up chair from the bathroom. After pushing the pile of clothes aside he put the chair in the closet and stood on it. Reaching up, he removed a thirty-inch square panel from the ceiling.

He hopped up, grabbed the edges of the opening and pulled himself into the attic space. A second later a light came on and Steve looked down at Val.

"Move back," he said.

Val took a step back and Steve dropped a blue back-pack to the floor.

"I'll bet you two-hundred grand it's not full of school books."

Val unzipped it and took out a stack of cash two inches thick, wrapped with an elastic band.

"Congratulations," she said, "you now move to the bonus round."

Steve hopped down.

"Let's get out of here," he said.

Val zipped the back-pack.

"Right behind you."

They looked at each other over the back-pack, which sat in the middle of Steve's desk.

"Okay," Val said, "we've got his money and that'll probably mess him up a little, but we're not done yet."

"No we're not," Steve said. "We need to do something to him that will guarantee Rhonda Cranston can live her life without having to look over her shoulder."

"May I suggest a car bomb?"

"I'd like to avoid that route, if we can."

"How about we tie a few nice thick steaks to his body and throw him in a pen with all those pit bulls?"

Steve grinned..."Let's keep that one on the back burner."

They sat in silence for a few minutes.

"What if we could send him to prison for life?" Val said.

"For what? Dog fighting? He'd be in and out in five years—if he was even convicted."

"What about murder?"

Steve frowned.

"Sure," he said, "if we can get him to murder somebody and then make sure he gets arrested *and* convicted."

Val smiled at him.

"We can make that happen," she said.

"How?"

"We get him to hold this..." she took her .45 out and held it up "...and get a witness to testify that Santoro threatened Fred Cranston."

Steve thought about it.

"That isn't totally crazy," he said. "In fact, it could actually work."

"Sure it could, that's why I said it."

"We just need to hammer out a few details," Steve said.

"Details? What details? We put the gun in his car. He finds it, picks it up and the cops are waiting for him. Fingerprints on a murder weapon—slam dunk. Throw in some incriminating testimony and before he knows what's happening he's the new dog at the nearest state pen and all his new friends are giving him bones."

"Good imagery, but you don't mind if we just massage the idea a bit, do you?"

"Massage away."

"Okay, it would be good if we could get him to do more than pick up the gun. The more prints on the gun, the harder it is for his lawyer to say it wasn't his. It would be good if we could get him to handle it, better if we could get him to load it—you know, so his prints are on the magazine and the rounds—best case scenario would be to get him to fire it."

Val looked at him with a furrowed brow, shaking her head.

"Do you think about everything this much?" she said. "I'm surprised you get anything done."

"I hate to say this," Steve continued, ignoring her remark, "but it's a shame we took Rhonda out of there. By kidnapping her, he created a link to Fred and he would have also been facing kidnapping charges."

"Well I'm sure she wouldn't mind if we let him grab her again. Hell, maybe we can get him to shoot her with my gun, then he'll be facing two murder raps."

"It'd be nice if we had somebody on the inside," Steve said. "One of the dog fight gamblers maybe."

"If we had played things differently with Buckshot we might have been able to flip him."

Steve looked at her and pointed a finger.

"What?" she said. "It was mostly a joke, I don't think Buckshot will be interested in helping us."

"I know it was a joke, but I think I have the next best thing."

~*TWENTY SIX*~

They used Val's rented Taurus to stake-out Brian Townsend's mobile home, since there was a fairly good chance Townsend had seen Steve's Jeep. Val checked her watch.

"It's going on two hours, it's dark and I'm getting hungry." she said. "So far your idea is batting exactly zero."

"Patience, grasshopper," Steve said without looking at her.

"Patience, my ass…" she began.

Steve sat up and pointed.

"Lo and behold," he said. "I give you the next best thing."

Val watched the scruffy-looking man leave the mobile-home and walk toward SR 100.

"Jesus," she said, "doesn't he have a shower in that rig?"

"Maybe he's trying to save the planet single-handedly by conserving water."

They followed at a discrete distance to a bar two blocks away called Poor Walt's.

"You ready?" Steve said.

"He'll never know what hit him," she said. "I'm not overdressed, am I?"

"Maybe a little," he said. "You don't have any holes in your jeans and you're wearing shoes, but it isn't very well lit in there so I think you'll be okay."

She pulled the door open and stepped inside. There were no windows and only enough lights to meet minimum lighting requirements.

Behind the bar, a round man with an old-fashioned handle-bar moustache, wearing a dingy tee shirt, stood with arms folded across his chest watching the lone television hanging from the ceiling. He straightened and tried to suck in his gut when he saw Val.

Brian Townsend sat by himself at the bar, and aside from two old men on the opposite side, was the only patron in the place.

Val took a seat next to him and held a hand up to the bartender, who was already walking toward her.

"Crown and ginger-ale," she said to him, "and give my friend here another one."

Townsend was already looking at her, trying to figure out why she had sat next to him, now he looked at the full bottle of Bud in front of him.

"I'm okay, Blackie," he said to the bartender.

Val smiled at him.

"Sorry," she said, "just trying to be friendly."

"We ain't friends," he said, "yet."

Blackie set a glass in front of Val.

"Take it out of this," Townsend said, holding up a twenty.

"Thank you, friend," Val said.

Townsend smiled at her with a combination of suspicion and curiosity.

"I told you," he said, "we ain't friends yet."

"Why not?" Val said. "You have enough friends?"

"Maybe."

She picked up her glass, holding eye contact with him while she gently sucked on the straw.

"Mama always told me you can never have enough friends."

"My mama told me never to talk to strangers," he said. "So either get to the point or go back where you came from?"

Val put her glass on the bar, holding eye contact with Townsend. She leaned in closer and smiled, touching his upper arm with her left hand while her right reached into her purse. Townsend looked down when he felt something touching his crotch.

"What the…" he said.

"Listen up," Val said with a smile, but in a soft voice only he could hear, "that's a taser and if I pull the trigger it'll send enough electricity into your balls to turn them into raisins. There's no windows in this place, so let's finish our drinks and leave together so we don't inconvenience these fine people with the smell of your burning flesh."

Townsend looked into her eyes, playing mental chicken.

"Go ahead, do it, how far do you think you'll get?"

Val looked at the bartender and the two old men.

"I don't know…maybe Cleveland?" she said. "Come on, Brian, you walk out with me and you look like some kind of stud. If you don't—well let's put it this way…the last time you had sex will be exactly that. The *last* time. I hope it was worth it."

Her eyes told him she was serious. He took a long pull from his beer and stood.

"Sweetheart, you got balls."

"And thanks to your wise decision," she said, "so do you."

"What the fuck is this shit all about?" Townsend demanded.

"We'll tell you all about it in a minute," Val said, sitting next to him in the back seat, the taser pressed against his leg. "Just relax."

"Brian," Steve said as he drove, "if you don't like what we have to say, we'll let you go, no harm, no foul."

Townsend looked at Steve's face in the mirror.

"Don't I know you?" he said.

"Not really, but we've crossed paths."

Steve drove around the corner to the Flagler Beach Pier. The three of them walked to the end and stood against the rail, out of earshot of a pair of night-fishermen and a couple sharing a romantic night on the pier.

"Brian," Steve said, "we need your help."

Brian's eyes widened and he looked from Steve to Val, then back to Steve.

"You need my help? And the way you ask is by putting a taser to my balls?"

"Sorry, it was the best we could come up with on short notice. Will you hear us out?"

"Well, what the fuck?" he said. "You went to all this trouble. Let's hear it."

"Okay, my name is Steve Salem. I'm a private investigator…"

"I knew you was a cop," Townsend said, "you're the guy came to my house the other day."

"Well, I'm not a cop," Steve continued, "I'm private. I'm working for Fred Cranston's wife, trying to find out who killed him. This is my partner, Val."

Townsend looked at Val, then back to Steve.

"Nice partner, watch your balls."

Steve nodded, "I will."

Val looked at Steve from behind Townsend and smiled, then mouthed the one-word question "partner?"

Steve winked at her.

"Anyway," he continued to Townsend, "I know you were involved with CJ Miller so I thought you might be interested in helping solve this case."

"Damn right, the cops from Daytona are looking at me, I don't need that shit."

"I know you don't, because I know you didn't do it. What we need is some help setting up the guy who did."

"Setting him up, how? You don't want me to wear a wire or some shit like that, do you?"

"No, nothing like that, but the cops couldn't find their asses with both hands," Steve exaggerated. "We want to give them the guy wrapped up nice and tight, so a lawyer can't get him off on a technicality."

By putting down the police and lawyers in the same sentence, Steve knew he'd struck a chord of sympathy. He let Townsend mull it over for a minute, then he delivered what he hoped would be the clincher.

"If you help us, it's worth a grand, no matter what. If it works five grand."

Townsend's eyes widened, but he didn't jump at the bait.

"How about twenty-five hundred for helping and ten if it works?"

Steve and Val had already discussed this part of the plan and, since they were using Santoro's money, were prepared to go higher, but they also didn't want to appear too anxious.

They looked at each other and pretended to silently discuss the terms.

"How about two if you help and seventy-five if it works?" Steve countered.

"I get the two in advance?"

"One in advance."

All right," Townsend said, "I'm in. What do I have to do?."

"The first thing we have to do is arrange for you to meet the mark, for that we'll need some help. Can we buy you dinner?"

~TWENTY SEVEN~

After they had been seated and their order taken, Steve excused himself and went to speak with Ralph Donabedian.

"You realize, of course," Ralph said, "that you're asking me to vouch for somebody I don't know to somebody I can't stand?"

"I do, Ralph," Steve said, "and I'm sorry to put you in that position, but if everything goes according to plan, it'll never matter."

Ralph inhaled slowly through his nose and looked toward the sky.

"You know how I earn a living," he said. "I do it by being on the right side of the odds. Now look around," he waved a hand in the air, "this restaurant is only one of the things the odds have secured for me. I say this because I want to know that even though I will do what you ask, I must also advise you that you are playing against the odds."

"I understand, Ralph, but I can't think of another way, so I'm at the mercy of the odds."

"The odds have no mercy," Ralph said.

Ike nodded.

"The only reason I'm agreeing to this is because I like you," Ralph told him, "and because you're doing it to help Fred's widow."

"I can't tell you how much I appreciate it, Ralph."

"Okay," Ralph said. "Ike will make sure the word is passed."

"Thank you."

Steve rejoined Val and Brian at the table just as their food arrived.

"We're all set," he said. "We start tomorrow."

They reviewed the plan over dinner, then drove Brian to his trailer.

"We'll pick you up around noon," Steve said.

"See you tomorrow, partner," Val said with a grin.

"I can hardly wait," he said.

After leaving Townsend, they drove to St. Augustine to check on Rhonda.

"How are you doing?" Steve asked her.

"I guess I'm okay," she said. "When can I go home?"

"With luck, you should be home in a few days."

"A few days? Why so long?"

"We have to be sure Santoro can't get to you."

"And how will you be so sure in a few days?"

Steve and Val shared a look.

"Well," Steve said, "it's probably best you don't ask too many questions."

"What about my cat?"

"Your cat?" Steve asked.

"Samson. I've never left him alone for more than a day."

"Does he have enough food and water to last a couple of days?"

"Sure, he has plenty."

"Fine. We'll check on him Thursday morning."

"But…"

"Rhonda," Steve placed his hands on her arms, below the shoulders, "cats can take care of themselves, you need to be more concerned about keeping yourself…safe."

Rhonda picked up on the slight hesitation.

"You were going to say *alive* instead of safe, weren't you?"

With no advance warning, she collapsed into his arms. Heavy sobs wracked her body and transferred the trembling to him. Realizing, for the first time, how terrifying the experience must be for her, he held her and let her get it out of her system.

When she began to calm down he led her into the cabin of the boat. It was the first time he had been inside and under different circumstances he would have taken a moment to admire it. Instead he led Rhonda to a sofa and sat down with her. Val went to the galley and made tea.

They drank tea quietly until Rhonda had calmed down. Soon her head slid onto Steve's shoulder and she was sound asleep. Steve carried her into one of the cabins and placed her in the bunk.

"I'll take that one, you take that one," Val said when he returned to the main cabin.

"What?"

We're staying here tonight," she said. "Deal with it. I'll sleep in this bunk, you sleep in that one."

"Yes ma'am," he said.

In the morning Steve was the first one to wake. He made coffee and waited on the stern deck for the women.

Val appeared twenty minutes later holding a cup of coffee. Ten minutes later Rhonda joined them.

"You didn't have to stay," she said, as she walked by him and touched his shoulder.

"It's okay," Steve said, "we didn't mind at all. In fact, I'd like to buy you ladies breakfast if you're interested."

"Don't have to ask me twice," Val said.

"That sounds nice," Rhonda agreed.

On the deck of a restaurant called Sandflea's, they enjoyed a picture-perfect Florida morning watching St. Augustine come to life.

After breakfast, they returned Rhonda to the boat and headed south on A1A toward Flagler Beach.

"I think she's forming a bond with you," Val said.

"What do you mean?" Steve asked.

"Little things, like the way she kept touching you, she sat next to you at breakfast and she looks at you like you're her savior."

"So what are you saying, she has a crush on me? Her husband hasn't been dead for a week yet."

"Not a crush, although I'm sure she's attracted to you, probably has been since the two of you met. No, it's more of a *knight in shining armor* thing. She trusts you, feels safe with you."

"I hope I don't let her down."

~TWENTY EIGHT~

"Rebs?" Townsend said. "That's the redneck dive out on 100—in the middle of nowhere, right?"

"That's the place," Steve said.

"Shit, that place makes Poor Walt's look like the fuckin' Ritz."

"At least," Steve said.

"So I'm going in alone?"

"No, Val will go with you. She'll pretend to be your girlfriend."

Townsend looked at Val admiringly and grinned, "Cool."

"I'll be pretending, stud," she said. "Don't punch above your weight."

"Are you going to remember your story?" Steve asked.

"Yeah, I got it, man. This guy Frank Cramden was my father..."

"Fred Cranston," Steve and Val corrected him in unison.

"Right, Fred Cranston was my father, but he split on my old lady when I was a kid, so I killed him last night..."

"Last Friday night," Steve said, Val put her hand over her eyes and shook her head.

"So I killed Cranston. Cranston's wife has three-hundred large that belongs to...what's this guy's name again?"

"John Santoro. And it's two-hundred thousand," Steve said.

Townsend waved a hand in the air…"yeah, yeah, six of one, seven of another."

"Ugh," Val said.

"Hey, how 'bout a break? I just learned this shit yesterday. You think you could do better?"

"In a coma," Val said.

"All right," Steve said, "let's reign it in. Val, lighten up on him a bit. Brian, you need to understand something—if Santoro even thinks you're bullshitting him, he'll kill you without thinking twice. You have to be believable."

"Okay, okay, I'll be believable."

They went over the story until they felt Townsend would pass muster.

"Okay," Steve said, looking at his watch, "Ike will be waiting for us, let's go."

Townsend drove Val's rental and Steve followed in the Jeep. One mile before Rebs they pulled to the side of the road where Ike leaned on his Harley, arms folded across his chest.

"Everything ready?" Steve asked.

"I'm here, ain't I?" Ike said.

Steve looked at Val and Townsend.

"Good luck," he said.

Ike fired up his bike and led the way. Steve stayed put and watched them drive away, hoping his idea wasn't a mistake.

Brian sang *Talk Dirty to Me* as they followed Ike to the door.

"That's enough of that shit," Ike said.

"Thank you," Val said, "he's been singing it since we got in the car."

"Everybody's got a fantasy," Ike said with a wink at Val.

"And for every fantasy, theirs at least one nightmare," she said.

"Hey," Townsend said, "what's that supposed to mean?"

Ike grabbed the door handle with his massive hand and looked at him.

"Forget about it, put on your game face."

The inside of Rebs was worse than Val had imagined.

"Don't know why I was expecting A-C," she said under her breath.

Ike grinned and led the way to the man sitting on a stool by himself. There were two other men in the place and a woman behind the bar. The air smelled like it hadn't been changed in months.

Santoro turned on his stool, stood and smiled, offering his hand to Ike.

"Hi, Ike," he said, completely out of character from the asshole Val had seen at the dog fights. "How you doing?"

Ike ignored the hand as well as the question.

"This is Brian, this is his old lady, Val," he said to Santoro, "this is John Santoro."

"How's it going?" Townsend said.

Santoro ignored him and spoke to Ike.

"You sure he's okay?"

Ike took his sunglasses off and looked sideways at Santoro.

"You sure you wanna ask me that?"

"No, no, Ike," Santoro back-pedaled. "Just making sure, I shoulda known. Tell Ralph…Mr. Donabedian he can trust me."

"I won't tell him a damn thing, it's up to you to prove it. You follow?"

"You bet, Ike. No problem here."

Although she couldn't voice it, Val was impressed with the respect Ike, and his boss, commanded from Santoro. It was a good thing to know and might be very useful if things started to get messy.

"I'll see you later," Ike said to Val.

"See ya," Brian and Val both said.

Val watched Ike walk out the door. When the door closed, she turned back to Santoro, who was looking her up and down as though he was considering buying her. She resisted the urge to pistol whip him. Instead she jerked a thumb at Townsend.

"He's the one here to talk to you, don't lose your focus."

Santoro rolled his toothpick from one side of his mouth to the other and sneered.

"Uh-huh," he said, then turning to Brian, "What's on your mind, punk?"

So much for the cordiality he'd shown Ike.

Steve was sitting in his Jeep listening to the radio when he heard the roar of a Harley approaching. Ike pulled to a stop next to him.

"It's out of my hands now," Ike said.

"Everything seem to be okay?" Steve asked.

"A maggot like Santoro, you never know. Luckily, he's afraid of Ralph. That ought to keep them alive."

"Great. Thanks Ike, and thank Ralph for me."

Ike threw a mock salute and popped his clutch. The Harley disappeared in a cloud of dust and Steve began waiting.

~TWENTY NINE~

Val waited for Townsend to speak, holding her breath and hoping he didn't blow it.

Townsend looked around the room, ignoring the woman behind the bar, his eyes paused when they saw the Pit-Bull in the corner. Then he looked at the two men on the other side of the bar. They were both bigger than him and even though one had a cast on his left arm, they looked like they could do some damage.

"I need to talk to you about something, uhh, you know, like secret," he said.

Val inwardly rolled her eyes. Santoro snickered.

"Secret? What the fuck is that supposed to mean?"

Townsend turned up his self-confidence a notch.

"It means I don't want to say shit in front of people."

Santoro eyed him for a second.

"Let's go outside," he said.

Thank God, Val thought.

The air outside was refreshing after the stale atmosphere of the bar.

"All right," Santoro said, "say what you gotta say, I'm busy."

"It's sort of a long story," Townsend said.

Val mentally crossed her fingers.

"My father was, uhh, a guy named…" his eyes flicked to Val, she held her breath, "…Fred, Fred Cranston."

Townsend grinned slightly, obviously proud for remembering the name, Val hoped Santoro didn't notice it.

"Fred Cranston?" Santoro said. "This is supposed to do what? Make me sad for you?"

"No, no, it's just, well he was my father but, like he didn't stick around after he knocked up my mother. You know? He split."

"My hearts bleeding here. Get to the point."

"My mother died in a car accident last year and I tracked him down, figured he owes me, you know?"

"He owed everybody."

"I know, right? That's what I'm getting at. I heard through the grapevine that he owes you two-hundred large."

This got Santoro's attention.

"You heard right. You here to pay me?"

"Sort of."

Santoro put his hands on his hips and exhaled thru his nostrils in frustration.

"Sort of? The fuck does that mean?"

Val was beginning to relax, slightly. So far Townsend was fairly convincing.

"What I mean is we can help each other. If you help me, I'll give you the money my father owed you."

"Help you? Help you, how?"

"It's like this, my father had a life insurance policy from his company, worth two-and-a-half million."

"And…"

"And…" Brian continued, "…if his wife is out of the picture, I'm his, what do you call it, sole…uhh…"

"Beneficiary," Val interjected.

Townsend pointed at her with his thumb.

"Yeah, so that means…"

"I know what the fuck it means, what does it have to do with me?"

Townsend shifted his weight and rubbed his face.

"I figure if you can get her out of the picture while I'm somewhere else, in front of lots of witnesses, that insurance dough is mine. I'll give you the two-hundred right off the top, plus a bonus. I'll take my money and go away, you never see me again." He clapped his hands. "Everybody wins."

Santoro locked eyes with Townsend for several seconds. Val began to get a good feeling.

"What sort of bonus are we talking about?"

He's hooked, Val thought. *We got him.*

"I'm thinking another two-hundred," Townsend said.

Santoro shook his head, but Val wasn't worried, some negotiation was expected.

"I'm thinking another five-hundred," he countered.

"Sounds good to me," Townsend said as a shocked Val looked on with her mouth open.

Santoro blinked.

"What if I said I was thinking another seven-fifty?" Santoro said.

Val made a show of stretching her arms over her head and took a few steps away to be out of Santoro's line of sight, then signaled to Townsend by slashing a finger across her throat.

"Uhhh, no," Townsend said, "your two-hundred, plus an extra five, that's my final offer."

Santoro grinned at him and nodded slowly.

"All right kid, you got a deal."

They shook hands and Townsend smiled with self-satisfaction.

"Great," Townsend said, "what's the plan?"

Santoro laughed.

"Well let me just pull one out of my ass," he said. "I don't have a plan yet you idiot. Give me your cell number."

Townsend took out the cell phone Steve had given him earlier and pushed a few buttons.

"386-555-2062."

Santoro entered it into his phone and put the phone back in his pocket.

"I'll call you tomorrow."

"How will I know it's you?"

"Answer the fucking phone and I'll tell you."

Without another word Santoro turned and walked back into the bar.

Townsend and Val got into the Taurus and drove away.

They drove past Steve as if they didn't know him, a precaution in case they were being watched. He followed them to The Golden Lion.

"So how did it go?" Steve asked.

"All things considered, it went very well," Val said.

"Very well?" Townsend said. "It went awesome."

"Don't hurt your arm patting yourself on the back, stud," Val said. "I almost feinted when you agreed to an extra five-hundred thousand without even blinking."

"What's the difference? We ain't giving him any money anyway, we could have told him five million."

"Not if we want him to believe us."

"She's right, Brian," Steve said. "Looking too anxious could have made him suspicious. Fortunately for us, he's more greedy and stupid than he is observant."

"What do we do now?" Townsend asked.

"We wait for him to call, and when he does you call me immediately."

"That's it?"

"That's it."

Townsend stood to leave.

"Then I'm gone, talk to you later," he said.

"I spoke with Rhonda while you two were with Santoro," Steve said after Townsend was gone.

"And?"

"I told her we'd go get her, take her out for lunch, bring her home so she can check on her cat—you know—get her off the boat for a few hours."

"Sounds good. When do we leave?"

"No time like the present."

"Works for me," Val said.

~THIRTY~

Brian's call came shortly after noon the next day.

"Looks like Santoro wants to get the ball rolling," Steve told Val after the call.

"I'm not surprised," Val said. "He's a greedy one."

"He wants Townsend to meet him at Rebs at 5:00 this afternoon."

"Should we have another sit-down with our boy first?"

"Yes, we most definitely should."

Forty-five minutes later they sat at a picnic table outside a hot dog joint near the pier in Flagler Beach. Brian plowed through his second hot dog while Val enjoyed a New Orleans Sno-Cone.

"Okay," Steve said to Brian, "Obviously Santoro has a plan. The most important thing for you to remember today is not to agree to it."

"I don't get it," Brian said. "I thought we wanted him to come up with a plan."

"We do, but we need to know what the plan is so we can make sure it will work for us."

"Work for us..." Brian nodded while chewing, "...you mean so he doesn't really kill Cranston's wife?"

"Keep your voice down," Steve said, nodding toward the building next door where a man and a woman were discussing landscaping ideas. "But yes, that's exactly the idea. We have to make sure that his plan can't succeed and, at the same time, make sure we can get him busted for Fred and CJ's murder."

"Got it," Brian said through a mouthful of hot dog. "I'll handle it. This guy killed CJ, I want him to pay."

"Good, and speaking of CJ, you can never let him know that you knew her. You didn't know her and you don't care about her. If the pieces don't add up, he won't think twice about killing you."

Brian nodded as he finished the last of his hot dog.

"Don't worry, I got this."

Santoro was leaning on the hood of his Trans Am when they pulled into the lot.

"Try to stay cool," Val said before getting out of the car. "Let him do the talking."

"Got it."

They walked across the lot to Santoro. At his feet lay Satan, the pit bull.

"Hey, man," Brian said "Nice dog."

Santoro looked down at Satan and nodded.

"Grand champion, retired," he said.

Val knelt to pet the animal. Upon closer inspection she noticed several scars around his eyes, neck and shoulder area—her hatred of Santoro elevated.

"I wouldn't do that if I was you," Santoro warned.

"You're not me," she said.

She remained still and made friendly sounds while Satan sniffed her hand. After several seconds the dog licked her hand and she began scratching him gently behind the ear.

Santoro watched, obviously confused.

"So he's a show dog?" Brian asked.

"Fighter," Santoro said, "trained him myself."

"Cool," Brian said. "Where'd he fight?"

"I know a place. Why, you interested?"

"I like to bet the ponies, dogs are just as good. Anyway, let's hear the plan?"

Santoro gave Val another leer before speaking.

"Maybe your broad should go fix her make-up or something."

Val restrained herself and remained in character as the good girlfriend. She placed a light kiss on Satan's forehead and stood up.

"It's okay, baby," she said to Brian, "I need to pee anyway."

Santoro watched her walk away with unabashed lust.

"Nice ass," he said to Brian.

"I'll say," Brian agreed. "So what's the plan?"

"Cranston's funeral is tomorrow, I assume you'll be there."

"Oh, yeah, sure," he said, "I'll be there."

"Good, there'll be lots of witnesses—you won't have to worry about being blamed. It's gonna look like an accident."

"What kind of accident?"

"You don't need to know the details."

"Yeah, I do," Brian said, bordering on demanding, "I'm giving you a shit-load of money, I want details."

Santoro rolled his toothpick around in his mouth and tried to stare Brian down through his sun glasses.

Brian stood his ground.

"All right," Santoro said. "This is how it'll go down. While the funeral drives over the intra-coastal a stolen pickup is going to side-swipe the car with Fred's wife in it. The car goes over the edge and into the water. Eighty foot drop—if she survives the fall, she'll drown before anybody can get to her."

"All right," he said, "as long as it looks like an accident."

Santoro put his hand out and Brian shook it.

"Just make sure you ain't in that limo," Santoro said.

"Right."

"So, you really interested in some action?"

"Oh, you mean the dogs?" Brian said. "Yeah, sure, I'd like to make a few bets someday."

"How about tonight?"

"Tonight? I can't tonight," Brian stalled, "I got something going on. Some other time."

"Suit yourself," Santoro said, "You got my number, call if you change your mind."

"Got it." Brian said.

"Brian, we went over this," Steve said as they drove to Brian's mobile home. "You weren't supposed to agree to the plan."

"I can't believe this," Val said. "Were you not listening or did you just decide exercise your right to be an idiot?"

"Fuck you," Brian said, "I wasn't thinking. When I remembered—it was too late to say no."

"Okay, don't worry about it," Steve told him. "It's not the way we drew it up, but we'll work around it. We just don't want him getting pissed."

"We also don't want him to succeed," Val said. "His plan actually has a chance of working.

"It would have a good chance of working if he were allowed to go through with it. Now we have to figure out a way to prevent that."

"I don't think he's going to change his mind," Brian said as he climbed out of the car.

"We'll figure something out, Brian," Steve said. "We'll pick you up tomorrow."

"This sucks," said Val as they drove away. "We need him to use the gun, not a stolen truck."

"I doubt Santoro will be in the truck anyway, he'll probably have one of his good ole boys to do it."

"That's even worse. Not only could his plan work, but he won't be there to take the blame."

"Then we'll have to ruin his plan," Steve said, "and make sure he uses one that suits our needs."

"We could try to get the funeral procession to changes its route," Val offered. "If they never go over the bridge..."

"Not much chance of that," Steve said. "The route from the funeral parlor to the cemetery is pretty straight forward. The only alternate routes would take them miles out of their way."

"What if we got Rhonda to ride in a different vehicle, instead of the limo?"

Steve thought for a second.

"I don't know," he said, "that could go bad in a hurry. If the pickup goes after the limo somebody else could get hurt, or killed. Besides, if they're watching, which they should be, they'll see which car she gets in to."

"That's it," Val said.

"What?" Steve asked.

"They'll be watching."

Steve sat up.

"And if they're watching, we can figure out who they are."

"Exactly."

~*THIRTY ONE*~

The Heaven's Gate Funeral Parlor sat between a small public playground and a gated neighborhood called Bulow Plantation.

At the entrance to Bulow, Steve showed his ID to the rent-a-cop in the guard shack and said he was investigating a cheating spouse within the community. The guard was more than happy to raise the gate after Steve allowed him to pry some sordid, albeit fictitious, dirt on the alleged perpetrator.

He found a vacant house whose back yard not only provided a clear line of sight to the funeral home and park, but also had an empty, in-ground swimming pool—perfect for cover. He walked into the pool at the shallow end and moved along until only his head was above the edge.

He took his binoculars out and waited.

The service was scheduled to begin at 10:00. Rhonda Cranston arrived at 9:00, accompanied by a middle-aged couple. Other guests began arriving at 9:30. Val and Brian showed up at 9:45.

Shortly after 10:15 a maroon Dodge pickup turned into the parking lot of the playground. Two men in their late twenties climbed out. One of them led a pit bull by a leash to the fenced-in area designated for dogs.

They took turns throwing a stick for the dog, but it was obvious their attention was focused on the funeral parlor.

Steve trotted to his Jeep and left the subdivision, waving at the guard on his way out. On his way to the park he took an aerosol can from beneath his seat and began shaking it.

The service was scheduled to end at noon, leaving him plenty of time.

He parked his Jeep behind the small building housing the rest-room facilities and attached a three-foot length of rubber tubing to the nozzle of the spray-can. Maintaining a casual appearance, he walked toward a spot behind the pickup, out of the line of sight of the two men.

When he reached the pickup he checked to make sure the men were still paying attention to the funeral home before dropping to his knees. He inserted the tube into the exhaust pipe of the pickup and pressed the button on top of the can.

When the contents of the can stopped flowing he withdrew the tube, stood and walked back the way he came. Once he was back in the Jeep he put the can of fast-setting foam insulation into the Home Depot bag and drove to the parking lot of a nearby bank where he dropped the bag into a dumpster.

Ninety minutes later the service ended and the guests filed into the parking lot where they lingered for several minutes before making their way to their vehicles. The two men gathered up the dog and climbed into the pickup.

By the time the procession got on the road it was almost 12:30, nearly two hours after Steve had injected the expanding foam into the exhaust pipe of the truck.

He called Val's cell phone.

"How did you do?" she asked.

"I emptied the can into the exhaust. It's had almost two hours to set up. Even if it hasn't fully hardened yet, just the sheer quantity of it should clog things up enough to do the trick."

"I guess we'll know soon enough," she said.

The last car of the procession left the parking lot and drove by the park.

"No movement yet," he said to Val.

The procession moved through the light at State Road 100 and still the truck remained where it was.

"It looks like…" Steve began. "Hold on."

The truck lurched backward out of the parking space, then started to move forward, but died after five feet. The passenger jumped out, opened the hood and peered in, shouting commands to the driver.

"Looks like they have mechanical problems. Where are you?"

"The lead car is almost to the bridge."

The two men stood at the open engine compartment for a couple of minutes before the driver took his cell phone out and made a call.

"These two won't be attending the service," he said.

"Cool beans," Val said, "see you later."

Steve hung up and watched the two men and their dog start walking away from the stolen truck.

"Sorry, boys," Steve said as he started the Jeep. "Next time, steal a more reliable truck."

He pulled away and headed for the cemetery.

~*THIRTY TWO*~

"Okay, Brian," Steve said, "now it's time to show us what you've got."

"What do you mean?" Brian asked, as he sucked the meat off a chicken wing.

"You need to call Santoro," Steve explained, "and convince him that you're pissed-off. Remember, even though *we* didn't want his plan to work, you need to convince him that you did."

Brian drained his beer and held the empty glass to the waitress.

"All right," he said, "I can do that. I can act pissed, easy."

"Another beer?" the waitress asked.

"Yeah," Brian said.

"He'll have a coke," Steve corrected.

The waitress walked away and Brian looked at Steve with annoyance.

"What the fuck, bro?" he asked.

"Don't bro me. Lives are at stake and one of them happens to be yours, I want you focused."

He leaned back in his chair and spread his arms.

"I'm focused, bro. I'm all there."

Val leaned across the table and spoke to him softly, but with no ambiguity.

"Don't make me take out the taser...*bro.*"

His smile faded and he picked up another chicken wing.

"All right, fine," he said. "When do I make this call?"

"As soon as you're done eating," Steve said.

Val looked at Steve, raised her eyebrows and made the sign of the cross as Brian dialed the phone.

"Hey, man," Brian said into the phone, "what the fuck happened? I never saw any fucking truck and the bitch is still breathing."

Brian listened for a few seconds.

"I don't give a shit...you're damn right you will...if you can't handle it let me know—I'll find somebody else who'll get it done."

Another pause.

"All right, if you say so. What's that? Where and when? Sounds good, I'll be there."

He disconnected and put the phone on the table.

"That sounded good," Steve said. "I even believed you."

"Can I have a beer now?"

Steve waved the waitress over and ordered a beer for Brian.

"Now tell us what he said."

"He told me the truck his boys stole shit the bed. Said there was nothing he could do about it and he'd take care of it."

"When, how?"

"Didn't say. He wants to talk to me tonight at the fights."

"Fights?" Val asked.

""Yeah," Brian grinned at her. "You and me are going to the dog fights tonight and I got a hundred dollar line of credit."

Val looked at Steve in mute protest.

Steve exhaled slowly and looked at Brian.

"You shouldn't have agreed to that without checking."

"What was I supposed to tell him? I had to ask my mother?"

"I can't..." Val began.

"You have to," Steve said.

"Take one for the team, babe," Brian said.

"If you call me babe one more time..." Val started.

"Come on," Steve said. "Let's focus. With any luck you'll be in and out of there quickly and we can put this thing to bed."

"It shouldn't take too long," Brian said.

"As soon as you accomplish three things," Steve said.

"Three?" Brian asked.

"Three," Steve said, holding up three fingers and counting them off as he spoke. "First, tell him that you'll give him the time and place we want him to make his move. Second, make sure he knows that you want him to do it personally, and third, give him the gun and the ammo."

"Is that all?" Brian asked. "You don't want me to get him to take a piss test?"

"If you can't handle it let us know now," Val said, raising her eyebrows. "We'll find somebody else who'll get it done."

"Easy, ba…" he began. "Just take it easy, I'll be there."

The gate was secured with a thick chain and an industrial strength padlock. Brian honked the horn twice as he had been instructed.

"Remember," Val said, "we're not here a minute longer than we have to be."

"Yeah, yeah," Brian said.

A man who looked to be about fifty pounds underweight unlocked the gate and waved them through.

"Y'all follow the road, go left at the fork and you'll see where to park."

"Thanks," Brian said.

They followed his instructions and parked in the clearing with the rest of the dog fighting enthusiasts. The majority of the vehicles were large pickups rigged for four-wheeling, but there were also several passenger cars, a few mini-vans and even one Jaguar.

"If we weren't here for something important," Val said as they walked through the parking lot, "I'd like to throw a few Molotov cocktails around."

"You got a mean streak, don't you?" Brian asked.

"Only when I see something wrong."

"This ain't wrong, these people aren't hurting anyone."

"Tell that to the dogs," she said.

They passed one of the fire barrels and entered the clearing. The crowd gave off an energy that bothered Val.

"You know, back in the day, people would gather in town squares for beheadings, hangings, even witch burnings. They treated it like a picnic—bring the kids, make a day out of it—like going to the beach. That's what this reminds me of."

Brian's demeanor changed as he scanned the crowd.

They stood at the outskirts of the activity, unable to see the actual fighting, for which Val was thankful. While she continued looking at the crowd with disgust, Brian searched for Santoro. A pair of men passed them, each one carrying video and audio gear, looking for a place to set up.

"I can't believe they're going to film this barbarism," Val hissed.

"There he is," Brian pointed, "let's go."

"Scum," Val said.

They worked their way around the edge of the action to one of the other fire barrels, where a small cluster of people stood around John Santoro—behind him stood the cages containing the upcoming contestants. People looked at dogs trying to figure out which one to bet on. One fat man punched the cages, maybe to determine the level of aggression of the dog inside. Santoro took bets and issued orders to the handlers.

"Look at him," Val said, "thinks he's Julius Caesar or something."

"More like the Godfather," Brian said. "Look at the fuckin' wad he's holding.

"I'd like to stuff it down his throat."

They waited in the fringes. After a few minutes, Santoro finished taking bets and worked his way to them.

"How's it going?" he said, rolling the toothpick around in his mouth and blatantly ignoring Brian to look at Val. She looked off into the night, feigning indifference and resisting the urge to kick him in the groin.

"Yo," Brian said, "you're business is with me, not my old lady's rack."

Val had to restrain herself from showing surprise at Brian's knack for role-playing. Perhaps she had misjudged him.

Santoro turned his head slowly, going for the tough-guy look, and snorted.

"Don't get excited, boy," Santoro said.

Brian moved into Santoro's space and looked deep into his eyes.

"You see a boy around here—you tie him to a tree and whip 'im...good."

After a brief stare down, Santoro backed up a step.

"Now, can we talk about how you're gonna solve my problem so I can get to bettin'?" Brian said.

"Yeah," Santoro said. "Let's do that."

After handing his roll of cash to another man and giving him instructions, Santoro walked away from the crowd, stopping after a few steps.

"She don't need to hear this," Santoro said, pointing at Val.

Panic struck Val when she thought about Brian being alone with Santoro again, but she knew it would be too risky to argue the point. She looked at Brian and gave him a curt nod.

"That's okay," she said, "I need to pee. Is there a bathroom somewhere?"

Santoro laughed and pointed into the woods.

"Yeah, fourth tree on your right."

Val turned and followed a path into the tree line as Santoro led Brian away.

Santoro stopped a few paces away and Brian resumed the offensive.

"Now what's your plan?" he asked.

"I'm gonna send my guys to her house tomorrow, they'll make sure she's home, make it look like a home invasion."

Brian rubbed his face with his hands.

"The same two guys that couldn't steal a decent truck?"

"That wasn't their fault."

"I don't give a shit—for the money I'm paying you, I want you to do the job personally."

"Me? Personally? I don't think so."

"Maybe you didn't hear me," Brian said. "It's you, or the deal's off. You start bringing in *your guys* and shit starts going wrong. Besides, I don't want any more links in the chain than we need, that way there's fewer people I gotta worry about keeping their mouths shut."

Santoro looked at him for several seconds, Brian stood his ground.

"All right, I'll do it myself."

"Good. Now there's two more things."

"Now what?"

"First, you won't find her at her house. She's staying with some friends for a couple days."

"Where do these friends live?"

"Uhh, I'll call you tomorrow with the address and time she'll be there."

"What else?"

Brian withdrew Val's .45 from his belt and a handful of bullets from his pocket.

"These are for you." He handed the gun to Santoro and dumped the bullets in his other hand. "Untraceable, use it and toss it when the job is done."

"I got guns."

"I don't care. Use this one."

"What's the difference?"

"I want her killed with this gun, I got my reasons."

Santoro shook his head slowly.

"If that's the way you want it, then I want you with me when I do it."

"What the fuck for?"

"You got too many rules, little man," Santoro said. "Ike and Ralph are only gonna buy you so much slack."

Brian ran a hand over his face, then put his hands on his hips.

"Besides," Santoro said, "if anything goes wrong and I get busted, you go down with me."

"Fine, I'll go with you, but you use that gun and those bullets."

"You're a weird mother-fucker," he said, "but if it means that much to you…"

"It does."

"Okay, you call me tomorrow and give me the time and place and we'll get it done."

"Fine. Now where'd my old lady go?"

~THIRTY THREE~

Partly out of curiosity, but mostly to avoid being near the carnage of the fighting pit, Val followed the path through the woods. The path ended at an area where the trees still stood, but all of the underbrush had been trampled away until the ground was packed and worn.

Each tree had a chain wrapped around the base, less than ten feet long and secured with a rusted padlock. There were small holes dug everywhere and the ground was littered with dog waste.

Her foot struck something heavy and she bent down to see what it was.

A dog collar with a five pound weight secured to it—next to it another collar with a seven pound weight and another with ten pounds.

"What the hell…" she whispered.

A short distance away she felt a distinct change in the ground beneath her feet. In the moonlight she saw an area about five feet square where the earth had been freshly dug and replaced.

"Hell is too good for this asshole," she whispered.

Having seen enough, she turned to head back to Brian. Crossing the clearing to the path, she followed it back the way she had come. As she rounded a bend in the trail she was startled by a figure approaching from the opposite direction. There was not enough time to hide or reverse course so she kept walking, hoping the person wouldn't question her presence.

"You lost?" the voice said.

Her stomach turned as she immediately recognized Santoro's voice.

"Oh, it's you," he said, moving much closer to her than she preferred.

"Yeah," she said, "I think I took a wrong turn."

"That's okay," he said, "I'll help you find your way out."

He moved in closer, their chests almost touching.

"Where's Brian?" she asked, trying to move around him.

"He's watching the fight," he said, stepping in front of her. "What's your hurry?"

She tried moving around him again, but he mirrored her movement, this time grabbing her arms and squeezing.

"Feels like you work out," he said.

"Let me go."

"I don't think so," he backed her against a tree. "I should be pissed that you were poking around back here, but I think we can work something out."

He spit his toothpick out, then leaned in and smashed his lips against hers, shoving his tongue deep into her mouth. The foul taste of liquor, mixed with God knew what else, caused her stomach to clench and she fought the urge to vomit.

She struggled to free herself, but she couldn't overcome his grip. She turned her head away and spoke loudly, hoping someone would hear.

"Let me go."

"Not til we get to know each other a little better."

He put his mouth against hers again, this time releasing his grip on her right arm to grope her breast.

Knowing she could not match his strength, Val's mind went from fight to flight. She remembered the taser in her purse and began moving her free hand toward it.

Santoro was too preoccupied with his assault to notice the movement.

She dug the taser out and felt for the on/off switch. As her thumb was about to switch the device on, he changed his position. In the shuffle, she lost her grip on the taser and it fell from her hand.

Santoro removed his hand from her breast and thrust it between her legs

As full-blown panic began to set in, Val heard a voice.

"Yo mother-fucker, what the fuck are you doing?"

Santoro released Val and turned around as Brian's fist connected solidly with his face.

The blow spun him around back to face Val, who ducked down, scooped up the taser and moved quickly behind Brian.

Brian stepped to Santoro and grabbed him by the back of the shirt, ramming his face into the tree.

"You're lucky I ain't poppin' a cap in your fuckin' ass right now. If you know what's good for you, you'll turn around, apologize to her and get the fuck out of my sight before I change my mind."

Santoro turned around and looked at Val. In the light of the moon she could see the fury in his eyes.

"She was looking for it," he said.

"You lying son-of-a…" Val started.

"Enough," Brian said, grabbing Santoro by the shirt. "We're leaving now, but the only reason I ain't killing you is because we still have business to do. I'll call you tomorrow."

He shoved Santoro away and stepped to Val.

"Come on, let's go," he said, putting his arm around her.

Val put a trembling arm around his shoulders and pulled him close.

"Thank you," she whispered as they moved along the path.

They reached the parking area and moved toward the car. A pickup pulled in and parked next to the Taurus, the driver jumped down and trotted around to assist the passenger out of the cab.

Just as her heart rate was beginning to slow down, Val felt it start to race again when she saw the passenger being helped from the cab of the truck.

His feet were bandaged almost to his knees and his face was swollen, but Val recognized Buckshot immediately.

She grabbed Brian, spun him around and kissed him. His arms wrapped around her timidly and he returned the kiss with confusion.

Val watched with one eye as Buckshot and the other man passed by, both of them grinning with perverse pleasure at the site of Val and Brian kissing.

When they were out of sight Val released Brian and moved to the car, Brian stood still for several seconds.

"Let's get out of here," she said.

He reached into his pocket for the keys and climbed into the car, looking at her with total confusion.

"I was just thanking you for what you did back there," she said.

Brian started the car.

"You're welcome," he said as he dropped the shift into gear.

~Thirty Four~

"The weighted collars are used to increase the strength of the dogs' necks," Steve explained.

"God I hate him," Val said. "You should have seen this spot where they chain the dogs to trees. There were no food dishes, no water dishes and there was dog crap everywhere. I'd like to chain him to a tree. Then there was a spot where the ground was freshly dug, no doubt where they bury the losers."

"Okay, Val, stay with us here. This is not the time to let this guy get under your skin," Steve said.

Val shook her head in disgust.

"I'll be all right," she said.

"You realize that what you did was an unnecessary risk, don't you?" Steve said.

The bartender placed a drink in front of her and she took a healthy swallow.

"I know, I know," she said, "I really didn't expect anything to happen, least of all…that."

"It's lucky Brian showed up when he did."

Val looked at Brian, who was being surprisingly modest about the whole thing.

"Thank you again," she said.

"Don't worry about it," he said.

"No, I'll worry about it. You saved me from unimaginable horrors, and after I've treated you like…well the way I did."

"Before you get too thankful, there's something I didn't tell you yet."

Steve and Val exchanged a look.

"What's that?" Steve asked.

"Well," he began, clearly nervous, "Santoro didn't like it when I told him about using the gun. He said the deal was off unless I went with him."

"What?" Steve said.

"That's lovely," Val said.

"I didn't know what to do, so I told him I'd go. I knew you'd be pissed, but I couldn't think of anything else and I figured you guys would be able to figure a way out of it."

"Nothing's leaping to mind," Steve said. "Let's call it a night, we'll sleep on it, if we can't figure something out by tomorrow afternoon we'll stall him."

Brian finished his beer and stood.

"I'm gonna split," he said. "Can one of you give me a ride home?"

Val handed him the key to the Taurus.

"We'll call you tomorrow," she said.

"There's more good news," Val said as Brian walked away.

She told him about the near encounter with Buckshot.

"Do you think he recognized you?" Steve asked her.

"Hard to tell," she said. "It was dark, his eyes were swollen and I grabbed Brian and kissed him to hide my face."

Steve nodded.

"If he did make you, he probably would have said something right away. We're probably safe."

"Let's hope so."

"Mind if I join you?" a voice asked.

They turned around to see Ike standing behind them.

"Sure," Steve said, waving to the bartender to get Ike a drink.

The bartender put a fresh bottle of Bud in front of Ike, but ignored Steve's money.

"So how's *Operation Santoro* going?" Ike asked.

"I wish I could say it was going without a hitch," Steve said, "but that wouldn't be completely accurate."

They explained the plan to Ike and told him about the complications.

"I wouldn't worry about Buckshot," Ike said. "Most of the time that ole boy is too high to recognize his own mama."

"Buckshot wasn't really worrying me," Steve said. "It's Santoro wanting Brian with him when he goes to kill Rhonda. Even though there won't be an actual murder, I don't like putting Brian in that position. The situation is too volatile—with a guy like Santoro too much could go wrong."

"Two days ago I wouldn't have cared," Val said, "but he saved my ass tonight."

"Then I think we need to figure out a way to return the favor," Ike said.

"We?" Val said.

Ike smiled at her.

"Sure, if that's okay with you guys."

"It's okay with me," Val said.

"I don't have a problem with it," Steve said. "I'm not proud. Problem is—whatever we do, we need to have a plan in place by tomorrow."

"Plenty of time," Ike said.

"Then you can have your boat back," Val added.

"Speaking of which," Ike said, "how's Mrs. Cranston doing?"

"She's fine, a little bored, but fine," Steve said.

"Why don't we pay her a visit and see if we can't relieve some of her boredom?" Ike said. "Little R&R will help us think."

"That's a great idea," Val said. "I could use a little R&R myself."

Steve looked at her. She raised her eyebrows and nodded quickly.

"Okay," he said, "let's do that."

"Ike asked me if I wanted to ride with him—you don't mind, do you?" Val said to Steve in the parking lot.

Trying not to look too surprised, Steve waved a hand at her.

"Of course not, go ahead," he said.

All the way to St. Augustine, Steve watched Val's hair flying in the wind as she clung to Ike like a child on a roller coaster.

At the marina, she hopped off the back of the Harley, grinning from ear to ear.

"Wow," she said as Steve joined them on the sidewalk, "that was unbelievable, I love it. I want to keep riding."

Steve looked at her and laughed.

"Do you mean to tell me that was your first time on a bike?"

"It was," she said, "and now I'm hooked. That's like a drug."

"It sure had a good effect on you," Steve said.

She hugged Ike, who smiled and returned the hug.

"Plenty of time for more rides," he said.

"Promise?" she asked.

"Cross my heart," he said.

"I called Rhonda from the road," Steve said. "She's expecting us."

They walked to the boat where Rhonda was waiting for them on the deck.

"Hi there," she said as they stepped aboard, "it's nice to have company."

She hugged Steve and squeezed him a little more than he expected, he returned the affection, realizing that he had missed her since they last spoke.

"Hi, Val," Rhonda said after releasing Steve, "Ike, this is really a beautiful boat."

"I'm glad you like it," Ike said. "Who wants a drink?"

"I'll have a beer," Steve said.

"I'd like a glass of wine, please," Rhonda said.

"I'll help you," Val said, bouncing after Ike.

Rhonda watched them walk into the cabin.

"Somebody has a crush," she said with a giggle.

"You think?" Steve said.

Ike and Val returned with a round of drinks, having taken a little more time than was probably needed.

Ike raised his bottle of Budweiser in the air.

"Here's to life going on," he toasted.

They toasted and drank, then settled into canvas deck chairs.

The marina was quiet and still. The conversation bounced from topic to topic, never focusing on anything specific for too long. By the time they were finishing their second drink, the four people, who were virtually strangers a week earlier, felt like close friends.

During a lull in the conversation Rhonda spoke.

"Steve," she said, "you failed to mention Ike was a hero."

Steve raised his eyebrows and shook his head.

"I didn't know," he said.

"Ike, please don't be angry with me," Rhonda said, "but I couldn't help but notice the Navy Cross and commendation hanging in the cabin. I recognized it because my father had one, from World War II."

"Oh, that," Ike said, trying to dismiss it. "That's nothing."

"Nothing?" Val said. "I doubt that. You were in the Navy?"

"Most of my life," he said.

"You were a SEAL weren't you?" Steve asked.

"Yeah, but it's all ancient history now. How about one more round?" Ike said, standing.

The others recognized his modesty and respected it. They agreed to another round of drinks and Ike went into the cabin again, with Val on his heels. When they hadn't returned after fifteen minutes Rhonda smiled at Steve.

"Do you think they got lost?"

"I'll see if they need some help," he said.

"I don't think they do," Rhonda said.

Steve opened the cabin door—before he got one foot inside he saw Ike and Val locked in a passionate kiss—Val standing on her toes to reach Ike. He did an immediate about face and rejoined Rhonda on the deck.

"Why don't we take a walk?" he said to Rhonda.

She laughed as she stood to follow him.

"I told you they didn't need help."

Just north of the marina, a row of horse drawn carriages stood at the sidewalk waiting for passengers.

"Would you like to take a ride?" Steve asked. "I promise I won't try anything."

She laughed and slapped his arm playfully.

"That sounds like fun," she said.

The driver of the carriage wore white tails and a felt top-hat. He welcomed them to St. Augustine, assuming they were tourists, and introduced himself.

"My name is Keith and my horse's name is Skywalker. We'll be your tour guides this evening. If you have any questions please feel free to ask Skywalker."

Steve and Rhonda laughed and Keith gave Skywalker a gentle nudge with the reins. The horse lifted his head and they were off.

Keith turned around in his seat.

"This your first time in the Nation's Oldest City?"

"No, we live here—Flagler Beach," Steve said.

"In that case, which version of the tour would you like? There's the *every detail imaginable* version, the *highlight version* or the *shut up, Keith* version."

Steve and Rhonda exchanged a glance and smiled.

"We'll take the *shut up, Keith* version," they said in unison.

Keith tipped his hat and smiled.

"Your wish is my command," he said turning to face front. "Looks like it's you and me again, Skywalker."

The ride took them on a beautiful scenic tour of St. Augustine, and even though they had both seen the city many times, the tour offered them a refreshing perspective.

"I really love this city," Rhonda said.

"Me too," Steve replied. "Reminds me of some of the older parts of Boston, only cleaner."

"I've never been to Boston," Rhonda said.

"It's a great city, I miss it sometimes."

"Sometimes?"

"Yeah, usually between May and October, that's when it's the best place in the world—great weather and the Red Sox."

The carriage ride lasted about forty minutes and when it was over neither of them were ready to return to the boat.

"How about a nightcap?" Steve suggested.

"I'd like that."

They crossed the street to a restaurant called Harry's.

"I hear this place is haunted," Steve said.

Rhonda clutched his arm as they climbed the steps.

"Will you protect me?" she asked.

They paused on the top step and looked at each other.

"I will," he said.

He opened the door and they stepped inside.

They sat at the bar on the second floor and enjoyed snifters of brandy.

So far the evening had been very enjoyable and, considering all that Rhonda had been through in the past week, she seemed to be keeping herself in good spirits. Steve made it a point to keep the conversation generic and light—avoiding anything that might risk bringing her down.

"How long have we been gone?" she asked as they strolled toward the marina.

Steve checked his watch.

"Almost two hours."

"I hope we won't be interrupting."

Ike and Val were sitting on the deck when they reached the boat.

"It doesn't look like we're interrupting," Steve said.

"Interrupting what?" Ike asked with feigned innocence.

"Yeah," Val said, "what are you implying?"

"Nothing," Steve said. "Nothing at all. Funny, I could have sworn you were wearing a different shirt when we got here."

"I was," Val said with a coy grin, "but I spilled some wine on it and Ike loaned me this one."

"Uh huh," Steve said.

After a few more minutes of light conversation, Rhonda yawned. "I'm sorry," she said.

"Quite all right," Ike said, standing. "Maybe it's time we hit the rack."

Val stood immediately.

"I agree," she said. "I'm beat."

Within minutes Ike and Val had disappeared into the main bedroom, leaving Steve and Rhonda alone on the deck. A small splash somewhere off the bow broke the silence.

Rhonda took Steve by the hand and led him to the other bedroom.

"Come on," she said, "there's two bunks in here. You'll be safe."

In the morning Ike treated them to breakfast.

When it was time to leave, Rhonda hugged Steve affectionately.

"Thank you for everything," she said.

"My pleasure," he told her.

"Why don't we meet at the Lion in two hours, throw some ideas around," Ike suggested.

"Sounds good," Steve said.

Ike kissed Val and roared off on his Harley. After returning Rhonda to the boat, Steve and Val drove back to Flagler Beach.

"You seemed to enjoy yourself last night," Steve said to Val on the ride.

"That's an understatement," she said.

"I don't know Ike very well," Steve told her, "but one thing I do know…he's not exactly the settling-down type."

"What makes you think it matters?"

Steve looked at her, slightly surprised.

"Sorry," he said, "I didn't mean to…"

"Forget it," she said. "It's very sweet of you to want to protect me, but I'm a big girl, I can take care of myself. Besides, we've got more important things to worry about."

"Yes, we do – I'll call Brian."

~THIRTY FIVE~

"Where is he?" Val asked.

Steve checked his watch.

"We told him to be here at noon, it's only ten after."

"We can get started without him," Ike said. "I think I have an idea."

"That's good news," Steve said, "because I haven't come up with anything."

"Here's the way I see it," Ike said. "Santoro may be a moron, but he won't make a play for Rhonda unless he's convinced there's no chance of witnesses and he can make an easy escape. Right?"

"Right," Steve said.

"For our part, we need to make sure that the location will allow Brian to get away before the cops show up to bust Santoro—and—we need to make sure Rhonda is never in any actual danger."

"Right again."

"How does this sound?" Ike said. "Brian tells Santoro that you'll be taking Rhonda to dinner tonight. After dinner you drive her to the home of the friends she's staying with, drop her off and leave. After you leave, she's alone in the house because the friends are out of town, perfect chance for Santoro's home invasion."

"Where might that house be?" Steve asked.

"Ralph owns a house—a couple miles up the road, ocean-side—we can use that."

"Excellent."

"Val and I are waiting in the house," Ike continued. "Rhonda comes in the front door, turns on a few lights and then we take her out the back door, across the yard, onto the beach, where we sit against the seawall and drink a glass of wine."

"I like that part," Val said.

"Meanwhile Brian and Santoro go in the front door and split up to search the house, except Brian doesn't search, he goes back out the front door and makes himself scarce. You've already called 9-1-1 and reported a break-in, so the police are on the way. Bob's your uncle, Santoro is caught breaking and entering, carrying the weapon that killed Fred Cranston. Rhonda testifies that he threatened her and before he knows what hit him, Santoro is up to his ass in convicts—literally."

They thought about it for a few minutes.

"One question," Steve said. "Why doesn't Brian go out the back and connect with you on the beach?"

"If he goes out the front, it's a sign to you that everything's going according to plan."

"So I take it I don't really leave after I drop her off."

"No you'll take up a concealed observation post."

"I think it'll work," Steve said.

"And it leaves room for improvisation if something goes wrong," Val said.

"Just a couple of concerns," Steve said. "First, Brian's fingerprints are on the gun as well as Santoro's, and since Brian has a record, he'll pop up when they run the prints."

Ike nodded and gave it a minute of thought.

"If he's questioned, Brian tells them he sold the gun to Santoro. It actually works in our favor, since there is no known connection between Rhonda and Brian."

Steve nodded.

"What about Val's prints? They're on the gun too."

Ike looked at Val.

"Have you ever been finger-printed?"

"Not me," Val said. "I'm a good girl."

"No military service, never applied at the Police Academy, worked in a bank?"

"No, no and no."

"Shouldn't be a problem," Ike said. "They'll be a set of unidentified prints on the gun, but since they catch Santoro *in flagrante delicto,* it won't matter.

"Now if Brian would get here, we could things started."

Fifteen minutes later Brian showed up.

"Did I miss lunch?" he said.

"Go ahead and order something," Steve told him, "we'll go over the plan while you eat."

They reviewed the plan several times, looking for potential flaws and making sure Brian understood his role.

"I got it," Brian said.

"Good. All that's left now is to call Santoro and get the ball rolling," Steve said.

"I'm ready," Brian said, taking his cell phone out and dialing.

"Hey, it's me," he said into the phone. "You ready to do this?"

Brian closed the phone and picked up his beer.

"All set," he said. "He'll be picking me up around 8:00. We'll wait for you to drop Rhonda off and then make our move."

"Good job, Brian," Steve said. "By this time tomorrow you'll have some serious walkin' around money."

"I hear that," he said.

He stood and finished his beer.

"I'll be right back," he said, "gotta go drain the lizard."

Ike stood also.

"I'm gonna go talk to Ralphy for a minute, let him know what's going on and get the key to the house. I'll be back."

Ralph sat at his usual table on the patio, by the stairs to the rooftop deck.

"Are you sure you want to get involved with this scheme, Ikey," Ralph asked.

"Yeah, Steve's a stand-up guy and he could use the help."

"I appreciate your attitude, and I certainly have no objection to helping Steve or to seeing that mutt, Santoro, get his just desserts, but be careful, there are wild cards involved—intangibles that can make a good plan go bad quickly."

"You mean Santoro?"

"Santoro is a loose-cannon for sure, but this young man posing as the insider is unpredictable and Salem's new partner could be problematic as well."

"Val? You think she's a wild card?"

"She did commit two murders. That in itself should give you pause, regardless of her motives. Another thing to keep in mind, she convinced Steve Salem, a man who usually wouldn't go through a stop sign, to help her frame somebody else for them."

Ike thought about it.

"Ike," Ralph said, "you're an incredibly intelligent guy, I'm sure you know what you're doing. I just want you to be careful."

"I'll be careful, Ralph."

Ike shook Ralph's hand and walked away. The restaurant manager approached the table and handed Ralph some papers to sign.

As Ralph signed the papers, Brian Townsend stepped out from behind the stairs and walked toward Steve's table.

~THIRTY SIX~

At 7:55 Santoro's black Trans Am rolled to the curb in front of the pier and Brian climbed into the passenger's seat.

"How's it going?" he said.

"Just fucking great," Santoro replied with heavy sarcasm. "You ready?"

Brian didn't respond.

"Hey," Santoro, said, "I asked you if you're ready."

"I'm here ain't I?"

Santoro checked his mirrors and pulled away. Several cars back, a black pickup followed.

"Okay, where's the house?" Santoro asked.

"Couple miles up A1A, number 1375."

"You sure about this set up?"

"Yeah, I'm sure. I talked to her this morning, she's going out with some guy named Steve, said she'll be home around 8:30. You got the gun?"

"I got everything I need," Santoro said.

Val and Ike sat on the sofa in the dark, waiting.

"So," Val said, "how do you feel about being a sheep dog?"

"A sheep dog?"

"Don't know that one, huh?" Val said.

"No, you'll have to brief me."

"There's a theory about people—it says there are basically three types of people in the world—sheep, wolves and sheep dogs. Most people are sheep, even if they don't know it. They live their lives with the rest of the sheep, they don't make waves—live and let live. If they hurt another sheep it's usually by accident. The wolves are the people who live for no other reason than to hurt and kill—predators. The sheep dogs are the people who protect the sheep, even if it means putting themselves in danger. They do it because they don't know anything else—they live to protect the flock even though they know the flock sometimes resents them."

Ike nodded.

"What makes you think I'm a sheep dog?"

"Well, first of all, you were in the military—that in itself pretty much makes you a sheep dog. You're willing to lay down your life to protect the flock, even if you don't know them. Second, there's your tattoo - *Death Before Dishonor* - with the image of a skull. The words say that you'll die for your beliefs, the skull says you're aware of your mortality and have accepted the fact that it is your destiny to die protecting those beliefs. How's that?"

Ike grinned.

"And here I just thought it was a cool tat," he said, "made me look like a bad-ass."

"Jerk," she said.

Before he could respond headlight beams shone through the window.

"Looks like it's time to get to work," Val said.

"Woof, woof," Ike replied.

Steve and Rhonda drove south on A1A toward the house.

"Are you okay?" he asked.

"I think so," she said. "I just can't wait until this is over."

"Soon."

"Not soon enough."

Steve slowed to turn into the driveway, waiting for oncoming traffic to clear.

"I'll walk you to the door and wait for you to go inside, then I'll leave. I'll drive around the block and stash my car, then come back on foot and hide nearby. Ike will call me when you're clear."

"Okay," she said, taking a deep breath.

"Remember to turn on a few lights at opposite ends of the house before you leave."

She unlocked the door and stepped inside, turning to shake Steve's hand before closing the door.

"See you soon," he said.

"I hope so."

Santoro and Brian sat in the driveway of a vacant rental home two doors south of the house.

"You're awful quiet," Santoro said.

"Who me?" Brian asked.

"No, I'm talking to the other guy in the car."

"Yeah, well, I just got a lot on my mind, that's all."

"Don't we all," Santoro said. "Looks like your meal ticket just got home."

Brian watched Steve's Jeep turn into the driveway. Steve walked Rhonda to the door and then drove off.

"That's our cue," Santoro said, starting the Trans Am's engine.

Without turning his headlights on, he coasted into the driveway and killed the engine.

"Don't slam the door," he told Brian as they got out of the car.

Rhonda turned lights on in the kitchen, the living room and the master bedroom along with the television.

Even though she knew Ike and Val were there, she was slightly startled to see them crouching in the shadows in the family room.

"Ready?" Ike said.

"I guess so."

"Okay, let's get it on."

He walked to the sliding door, opened it and let the women pass through before closing it behind him. Val was already leading Rhonda across the yard to the stairs. At the bottom of the stairs they walked south on the beach and sat in front of the seawall two houses away. Ike called Steve.

Steve walked quickly back toward the house, keeping in the shadows as much as possible. He found a spot behind a tall palmetto bush to wait for Ike's call.

The phone vibrated less than a minute later.

"Yeah," he answered.

"Amity station, this is the Orca," a voice said, "we have Mrs. Brody."

"What?" Steve said.

"Oh come on," Ike said, "don't tell me you've never seen Jaws."

Steve let out a nervous laugh.

"Are you telling me you have Rhonda?"

"Safe and sound, make the call."

"Right."

He hung up the phone and dialed 9-1-1.

"Hi," he said to the operator, "I was walking my dog on A1A and I saw two men break into a house, then I heard a woman scream. Yeah, it's right on A1A, number 1375. Do I have to give my name? I don't really want to get involved."

He disconnected the call, turned the burn-phone off and tossed it into the woods behind him. He took his own phone out, and called Ike.

Santoro placed a hand on the door knob and turned it slowly. Brian watched, subconsciously holding his breath. The knob turned and they stepped into the foyer. There were lights on at each end of the house and noise from a television coming from the left end.

"I'll check that end," Santoro said quietly. "You look that way."

Brian moved off to the right slowly while Santoro went left. Brian turned and watched Santoro go into the room at the opposite end of the house, then he retraced his steps to the front door.

As quietly as he could, he turned the knob and slowly opened the door. He let out an audible yelp when he saw the swollen face of a man grinning at him from beneath a black hood.

"Goin' somewhere?" the man asked.

"Okay," Steve said to Ike. "The cavalry is on the way."

"Cool," Ike said. "Tell them not to make too much noise, we're trying to enjoy some wine here."

"I'll mention it to them…" he paused, "…what the hell?"

"Something wrong?"

"There's a guy walking into the driveway."

"Cop?"

"Definitely not."

"What's he doing?"

"Walking to the front door. I can't get a good look at him, he's got a hoodie on."

"Give it a minute," Ike said. "Could be a neighbor looking for his poodle."

"Brian just opened the front door, he looks shocked...shit."

"What?"

"The guy pulled a gun and pushed Brian back inside the house. Now he's closing the door. Uh-oh, this is bad..."

"Now what?"

"I just saw the guys face as he turned around to close the door."

"And..."

"It's Buckshot."

Instinct told Brian to be afraid, the sight of the revolver in the man's hand confirmed it.

"Back the fuck up," the man ordered.

Brian did as he was told, raising his hands in the classic *I surrender* position.

The man removed his hood then turned and looked into the driveway to see if he had been followed. Satisfied, he closed the door.

"Who are you?" Brian asked, temporarily forgetting about Santoro.

"His name is Buckshot," Santoro said from behind, "and if you don't want him to put a hole in you, you better start talking. There's nobody here, which you probably already knew, this looks like a damn set-up to me."

"Whoa, easy bro," Brian said. "I'll tell you the whole story, but not until we get out of here."

"You listen to me, punk," Santoro said, taking out the .45 Brian had given to him. "We'll stay right here until you tell me what the hell is going on. That piece of tail you call your old lady was hanging with a private dick. He was asking questions about Fred Cranston. They tied Buckshot to a telephone pole and let him get eaten up by fire ants, made him talk about me and Cranston and my money. Then you show up with the same broad, saying Cranston was your old man. What the fuck is going on?"

"Listen, I'll tell you the whole story, I got no use for those people, but if we don't get out of here right now, we're all gonna be talking to the cops."

Santoro glared at him for several seconds.

"Come on, man," Brian said, "we don't have much time. You gotta believe me."

"All right, let's go—but if you're bullshittin' me I'm gonna fuck you up, bad."

"Can you go back and see what's happening?" Steve asked Ike.

"I could, but any minute now Flagler Beach's finest will be here, maybe we should let them handle it."

"What about Brian?"

"What about him?"

"I'm not crazy about hanging him out there like that."

"We'll have to let it play out and deal with the aftermath, we don't want to be present when the law arrives," Ike said

"Hold on," Steve said. "The door's opening again. They're coming out, Brian first, with Buckshot behind him and Santoro in the rear. They're making Brian drive the Trans Am, Santoro is getting in the passenger's side and Buckshot is walking down A1A. The Trans Am is leaving and there goes Buckshot in his truck."

"Looks like the party's over," Ike said. "Let's get out of here."

"I'll get the Jeep and pick you up."

"We'll be walking south on A1A."

The police showed up just as Steve hung his phone up. He trotted to his Jeep and picked the others up four houses south and drove to his office.

~THIRTY SEVEN~

Santoro grabbed Brian by the throat and slammed him into a tree.

"Now tell me what the fuck is going on or I'll take you over there and feed you to the dogs," he growled.

"Let go of my throat so I can talk," Brian croaked.

Santoro dropped his hand and looked at Buckshot.

"If he moves…" he said.

Buckshot nodded and cocked the hammer on his revolver.

"Now start talking," Santoro said to Brian.

Brian rubbed his throat and took a breath.

"The whole thing was a set-up," he said. "They were trying to frame you for doing Fred Cranston."

"How were they gonna do that?"

Brian nodded at the .45 tucked in Santoro's belt.

"That gun is the one that killed Cranston, your fingerprints are all over it, and they're on the bullets and the clip too. They paid me to feed you the story about my step mother so they could set a trap at the house. If we didn't get out of there when we did you woulda been busted for murder."

"That's why you were trying to leave?"

"Right, I was supposed to split before the cops got there."

"So why shouldn't I kill you? You were in on it—you were helping them set me up."

"I was, but only because they were paying me. I don't even know them."

"So how'd you get in with them?"

"They came to me—put a friggin' taser to my balls. Told me that you killed Fred and CJ..."

"CJ? Who the hell is CJ?"

"She was my old lady—my real old lady. They said you killed her and they wanted me to help them put you away."

"Well, I didn't kill nobody."

"I know that now. It was her, Val—she killed both of them."

"Why?"

"How the fuck do I know? All I know is me and you got a reason to work together. I want payback and you want your money."

"What the hell do I give a shit about your payback? I should just waste you before I go after them."

"You waste me and you won't ever get your money."

"Why not?"

"Because they think I'm on their side, you kill me and that'll just give them another reason to come after you. Or you can use me to trade for your money. You get your money back and throw me five-grand, we all walk away happy—as long as I get to waste Val."

Santoro considered it. Brian threw in another piece of incentive.

"And another thing—that guy Ike is itching for an excuse to take you out."

Santoro paced in circles, the toothpick in his mouth rolling from side to side rapidly.

"Fucking Ike," he said, "what'd I ever do to him?"

"I can't believe that son-of-a-bitch was a step ahead of us," Ike said. "Now I'm pissed."

"It wasn't your fault, Ike," Steve said. "It had to be Buckshot."

"I didn't think he saw me," Val said, "but I guess he did."

"What do we do now?" Rhonda asked.

Nobody answered.

"For the first time in twenty-four years," Rhonda said, "I want a cigarette."

"We have to be pro-active on this," Ike said. "We have to figure out where Santoro would go and we have to hit him before he has a chance to plan his next move."

"We know where he'll go," Val said.

Ike looked at her, then to Steve.

"She's right," Steve said.

"Then let's go," Ike said.

"What about me?" Rhonda said.

"You can wait here," Steve said.

"Alone?"

"I'll stay," Val said.

Ike looked at Steve.

"What do you have for weapons?"

"We gotta figure out a plan," Santoro said.

Brian picked up a wooden pole and twirled it as he watched Santoro pace.

"You shouldn't play with that," Buckshot said.

"Why, what is it?"

"It's called a bang-stick," Santoro said, taking it from him. "Like a cattle prod, it's for training the dogs."

Santoro put the end of the stick in front of Brian's face.

"You wanna see how it works?"

"Christ, no," Brian said. "What the fuck is it with people wantin' to electrocute me?"

"Relax," Santoro said as he walked to a dog chained to a nearby tree, wearing one of the weighted collars.

The dog growled as Santoro approached, Santoro touched the end of the stick to the dog's hind quarters. There was a short snap and buzz followed by a yelp.

"See?" Santoro said with a laugh. "Works good, huh?"

Brian nodded.

"Great," he said.

"All right, now we still need a plan."

"Why don't you call Steve, tell him you'll trade me for the money and tell him to have Val deliver it."

"Just like that?"

"Sure, why not?"

Santoro walked by the dog again, drawing another growl. He hit him with the bang stick again, another yelp.

"Fuckin' mutt," he said. "Growl at me."

After ten more minutes of pacing and a few more shocks to the dog, Santoro stopped pacing.

"Fuck it," he said. "We'll have to use your plan, I can't think of shit."

Brian opened his phone and pressed a couple buttons, then handed it to Santoro.

"Just hit send."

Santoro looked at the phone, then Brian, then back to the phone.

"Here we go," he said as his thumb pressed the send button.

When his phone rang Steve was just turning into the same parking lot he and Val had used on the night they first visited the junk yard.

"It's Brian's phone," he said to Ike.

"Just go along with him," Ike said.

Steve answered the call, putting it on speaker.

"Brian?" he said.

"No, asshole, it ain't Brian, and if you don't want Brian dead you'll shut up and listen."

"Take it easy, I'm listening."

"You got my money, I got your boy. Even trade, everybody's happy."

"Sounds fair, where and when?"

"Rebs, in an hour, the broad delivers the money—alone."

"Give us an hour-and-a-half, I have to pick up the money."

"If she's ten seconds late I'm wasting this punk."

"Let me talk to him."

There was a shuffling sound as Santoro passed the phone to Brian.

"Yo."

"Brian, you okay?"

"I'm good."

"Sit tight, we'll get you out of there soon."

The line went dead.

Steve and Ike walked along the railroad tracks.

"There are four trailers out by US 1, when he took Rhonda he kept her in one of them, that's probably where Brian is," Steve said.

"I doubt it," Ike said. "That call was made outside. I heard a dog bark and an owl screech."

"They must be by the fighting pit."

Santoro's Trans Am and Buckshot's pickup were the only vehicles in the parking area. They heard low muffled conversation from the pit area. Ike pointed to the far side, instructing Steve to circle left. Ike circled to the right.

"We got some time to kill, might as well go out to the trailer and get comfortable," Santoro said. "Where'd Buckshot go?"

"I'm taking a leak," Buckshot called from the trees.

"Hurry up, these bugs are driving me crazy," Santoro yelled.

Using the sound of Buckshot's voice to pinpoint his location, Steve crept up behind him as he relieved himself. He pressed the barrel of his gun against Buckshot's head.

"Don't do anything stupid, Buckshot, just finish and zip up."

Buckshot zipped his pants and turned around with his hands up.

"Wow," Steve said looking at Buckshot's swollen face. "Maybe you're allergic to fire ants after all. Now let's go, and keep it quiet."

Buckshot led Steve along the path toward Santoro.

"Come on, Buckshot," Santoro called, "how long you gonna take?"

When Buckshot failed to respond, Santoro drew his gun.

"Buckshot?"

No answer.

"Buckshot, answer me."

Buckshot glanced over his shoulder at Steve.

"Just keep moving," Steve whispered.

Buckshot stopped, Steve raised his gun...

"Get out..." Buckshot yelled.

Steve slammed the butt of his gun down onto Buckshot's neck—dropping him unconscious to the ground—then moved off the path into the trees and toward Santoro.

"Mother fucker," he heard Santoro say before a shot rang out.

Steve kept moving, coming out of the trees to Santoro's left, he stepped into the clearing pointing the gun.

"Drop the gun," he said.

Santoro let the gun fall to the ground, Brian scooped it up.

"You okay, Brian?"

"I'm fine."

Santoro took advantage of Steve's momentary lack of attention and lunged at him. They fell to the ground, Steve's gun flying into the trees.

Brian raised the gun and fired.

Santoro jumped up and ran while Steve clutched his right leg.

"Brian, drop the gun," Ike yelled.

Brian dropped the gun, Ike moved over and picked it up.

"You all right?" he asked Steve.

"Through and through, I'm okay," he said. "Get Santoro."

Ike took off into the woods.

Santoro ran through the woods, twigs slapping his face, briars pulling at his legs.

He turned to look behind him for signs of pursuit and his legs got tangled in brush, sending him tumbling into a cactus bush.

Ignoring the pain, he staggered ahead to the clearing. His foot struck something heavy, sending him tumbling to the ground. His face landed on something soft and moist—the smell left little doubt as to what it was. Looking back to see what his foot had hit, he saw a ten pound weight fastened to a dog collar. The urgency of his situation overruled his urge to clean his face and he began to pick himself up to continue his escape.

That was when he heard the low, steady growling.

The last thing he saw was the wide open mouth of an eighty-pound pit bull lunging at his throat—a five pound weight hanging from its collar.

Ike burst into the clearing as the screams turned into a sloppy, gurgling sound. Santoro's life bled out onto the hard-packed dirt and soon the only noise was that of a dog growling, combined with the sound of ripping flesh.

Ike turned and walked back to Steve.

~THIRTY EIGHT~

Val pounced on Ike and hugged him fiercely when they walked into the office.

"Is it over?" Rhonda asked.

Steve limped in, followed by Brian.

"It's over," he said.

"Santoro?" Val asked.

"He won't be a problem to anybody, ever again," Steve said as he went to the bathroom, coming out a minute later with a first aid kit and sitting in a chair.

"Are you okay," Rhonda and Val asked in unison.

"I'm fine," he said.

Ike put the .45 on Steve's desk and knelt next to him to help dress the wound.

"You're pretty good at that," Val said.

"Wish I could say I'd never done it," he said.

"Is he going to be all right?" Rhonda asked.

"He'll be fine," Ike said. "Not much more than a scratch."

"Tell that to the pain," Steve said. "It's a good thing Brian wasn't aiming higher."

"Brian shot you?" Val asked.

"Easy, Val," Steve said. "He was aiming at Santoro—it was an accident."

"Then why is he pointing that gun at us?" Rhonda asked.

"You fuckin' people are some real shit," Brian said.

He held the gun up, moving it back and forth, covering each of them.

"Easy, Brian," Ike said, moving to stand.

"Just stay there," Brian yelled, pointing the gun at him.

Ike knelt down, facing Brian, his back to Steve. He casually lifted the back of his shirt allowing Steve to see the Colt tucked in his belt.

Brian spoke to Val.

"I heard Ike talking to the guy in the wheelchair, I know what you did. Tell me why?"

"Fred Cranston killed my father," Val said. "And then stole his identity. He was…"

"Why CJ?" Brian said, his voice thick with emotion.

"Brian…" Val started.

"You killed CJ and thought it was okay to use me to frame somebody else for it? Who the hell do you think you are?"

Val said nothing, just shook her head.

"You had your beef with Fred Cranston, but killing CJ was wrong, she never did anything to you," he said.

"I'm sorry, Brian," she said. "It's not fair."

"Not fair?" he said. "That's all you can say?"

Steve slowly began withdrawing the gun from Ike's belt.

"Ever since you met me you've acted like you were better than me," Brian said.

He stepped closer to her.

"You thought you had the right to deal justice…well, I guess if it's okay for you, it's okay for me, right?"

"Brian…" Val said.

He stood directly in front of her.

"Brian," Steve said raising the Colt.

Brian leveled the gun at Val's face.

A click filled the room and the magazine of Val's .45 fell to the floor. Brian racked the slide, ejecting the round from the chamber.

He put the gun on the floor in front of her and walked to the door, turning to face them after he opened it.

"I guess this makes me better than you after all," he said before walking off into the night.

Ike grabbed the gun from Steve and sprinted toward the door.

"Ike wait," Val said. "Let him go"

Ike stopped and looked at her. She looked back at him, eyes watering.

"Just let him go."

~*THIRTY NINE*~

Val stared straight ahead, no expression, eyes watering.

Ike was the first to speak.

"Val, I spent the majority of my life doing things that most people would find reprehensible, and I've been told many times about what a horrible person I was for doing them."

"Are you trying to make me feel better?" Val said through her tears.

"Not really, I'm just trying to help you deal with what just happened."

"It's a little different, you were in the military…you did what you did because it was the right thing to do."

"Only according to the people who told me to do it," he said. "But if they had told me to do something I didn't believe in, it would have been a different story."

"What are you saying?"

"Laws and rules are important, but they're not perfect. There are times when our sense of right and wrong doesn't jive with what the law says."

"That doesn't make it right to become a vigilante."

"Maybe not, but twenty-some years ago two people got away with a murder—a murder committed solely for greed. Call it vigilantism if you want, but your action corrected that wrong - regardless of what you call it."

"Okay, so what are you telling me? That Brian was wrong about justice? That I should never feel guilty about what I did? Because I don't know if I can do that."

"No, that's not what I'm saying at all. I'm trying to give you a way to live with it. Think of it like a cosmic checkbook. In the end the checkbook has to balance—regardless of the law."

Val nodded, her eyes still wet with tears.

"I understand what you're saying, but I don't think I'll get over this anytime soon."

Ike grinned.

"I didn't say you'd ever get over it, I said you'll learn to live with it."

~EPILOGUE~

Steve sat at his desk, catching up on paperwork on a quiet Wednesday morning.

The stillness was interrupted by the roar of a Harley outside, followed by the front opening.

"What are you going to do when it rains?" he asked.

"Call you for a ride," Val said. "This is Florida, I don't need a car."

"Hard to believe you'd never even ridden on a bike until four months ago," Steve said. "Now you've got your license and a brand new Harley. What other influences has Ike had on you?"

"Can't tell you—or I'd have to kill you," she said as she put her helmet on top of the file cabinet behind her desk. "Any coffee?"

"I just made a fresh pot."

"Thank God…late night."

"On a Tuesday?"

"Don't be a hater just because you're not young anymore."

Val went into the kitchen and fixed a cup of coffee then walked to her desk.

"Anything interesting this morning?" she asked. "Oh my God, this coffee is terrible. Something has to be done."

"I should have made it a condition of employment that you had to buy a new coffee maker."

"I would if you paid me."

"Hey, we had an agreement," Steve said. "After giving half of Santoro's money to Rhonda, paying a few expenses and making a donation to the Flagler Humane Society, you could keep the rest—and you didn't draw a salary until we got our first case."

"Well I didn't think we'd be going four months without a case."

"I hate to break it to you, but I've gone as much as six months," he said.

Val opened her mouth to speak, but was interrupted when the front door opened.

"Did I come in the middle of something?" Rhonda asked as she entered the office carrying a bag from high-end retailer Brookstone.

"No," Steve said as he stood and kissed her. "We were just reviewing the terms of Val's employment."

"Again?"

"She forgets." Steve said. "What's in the bag?"

"I was in the mall last night and I bought you a gift."

"Wow," Steve said. "You didn't have to do that."

"Well it's for both of you," she said.

Val bounded around her desk and took the bag from Rhonda.

"I get to open it," she said.

Val pulled a box containing a new coffee maker from the bag.

"Oh, sweet. Rhonda, you rule."

"You two planned this," Steve said.

Val was already in the kitchen opening the box and setting up the new appliance.

"It wasn't planned," Rhonda said as she slid her arms around him and kissed him. "We've been dating for almost three months—I've had your coffee."

"Oh, that's just hurtful," Steve said.

"You tell him, Rhonda," Val called from the kitchen.

Before Steve could respond the phone rang.

"Salem-Casey Investigations," he answered.

Rhonda went to the kitchen to help Val while Steve handled the phone call.

"I'm still pushing for a name change," Val said. "Salem-Casey is so boring. I suggested Val-halla but it was shot down in committee."

Val was pouring water into the coffee maker when Steve entered the kitchen.

"Our first pot of good coffee should be ready in about seven minutes," she said.

"It'll have to wait," Steve said. "We have to go interview a client."

"Are you serious? Four months of nothing—we finally get a good coffee maker and now we have a job?"

"Sorry, that's the way the bean bounces."

"I'll take it," she said. "What's the job?"

"The client is a woman named Joyce Donahue, her husband's been missing for a week. She filed a missing person's report but the Flagler Beach PD just doesn't have the manpower to conduct a full-blown search."

"What do we know about the husband?"

"Patrick Donahue," Steve read from a pad, "68-years-old, retired Architect from Rhode Island. Works as a part-time consultant to a local Architectural/Engineering firm, loves fishing and golf, volunteers for a local charity called Christmas Come True and, according to Joyce, didn't have an enemy in the world."

"He had at least one," Val said.

"Does this mean you won't be available for lunch?" Rhonda asked.

"I'll call you," he said.

Val stood by the open front door.

"Let's go, my first paycheck is waiting."

STEVE AND VAL WILL RETURN IN THEIR NEXT CASE

LIQUIDATED DAMAGES

SCHEDULED FOR RELEASE IN EARLY 2013

IF YOU ENJOYED BACKSEAT TO JUSTICE PLEASE FIND THESE OTHER TITLES BY TIM BAKER:

Living the Dream - Kurt's grand kidnapping scheme might work if it doesn't kill him first.

Water Hazard - Steve Warwick buys some used CDs, but didn't bargain on murder.

No Good Deed - Kurt is back and trying to do the right thing, but Karma didn't get the memo.

Pump It Up - thanks to Ernie Boudreaux's back room proceedures beauty is now six feet deep.

For more information, links and sneak previews visit www.blindoggbooks.com

Made in the USA
Columbia, SC
14 October 2022